But [...] interest [...] just might not be his id[...] ideal woman. In fact, a cop probably wouldn't even be a contender.

Even if Wynn turned out to be delighted she was a cop, there was still the little matter of Mike. Maybe he didn't like kids. Or maybe he thought little kids were cute, but drew the line at big-mouthed twelve-year-olds, for which she wouldn't blame him.

The effect the rest of her family might have on him she didn't even want to contemplate.

And yet, with all the difficulties she could foresee, Wynn was too good to just give up on. Terry hadn't thought she'd ever fall in love again. That love now seemed like a gift, and she wanted to hold it and treasure it....

ABOUT THE AUTHOR

Beverly Sommers likes living alone, traveling alone, neon palm trees and red furniture.

Books by Beverly Sommers

HARLEQUIN AMERICAN ROMANCE

11–CITY LIFE, CITY LOVE
26–UNSCHEDULED LOVE
62–VERDICT OF LOVE
69–THE LAST KEY
85–MIX AND MATCH
125–CHANGING PLACES
137–CONVICTIONS
152–SNOWBIRD

HARLEQUIN INTRIGUE

3–MISTAKEN IDENTITY

These books may be available at your local bookseller.

Don't miss any of our special offers. Write to us at the following address for information on our newest releases.

Harlequin Reader Service
901 Fuhrmann Blvd., P.O. Box 1397, Buffalo, NY 14240
Canadian address: P.O. Box 603,
Fort Erie, Ont. L2A 9Z9

Le Club
BEVERLY SOMMERS

Harlequin Books

TORONTO • NEW YORK • LONDON
AMSTERDAM • PARIS • SYDNEY • HAMBURG
STOCKHOLM • ATHENS • TOKYO • MILAN

To Wendy, the best-looking blonde at Le Club.

Published September 1986

First printing July 1986

ISBN 0-373-16165-4

Copyright © 1986 by Beverly Sommers. All rights reserved.
Philippine copyright 1986. Australian copyright 1986.
Except for use in any review, the reproduction or utilization of
this work in whole or in part in any form by any electronic,
mechanical or other means, now known or hereafter invented,
including xerography, photocopying and recording, or in any
information storage or retrieval system, is forbidden without
the permission of the publisher, Harlequin Enterprises Limited,
225 Duncan Mill Road, Don Mills, Ontario, Canada M3B 3K9.

All the characters in this book have no existence outside the
imagination of the author and have no relation whatsoever to
anyone bearing the same name or names. They are not even
distantly inspired by any individual known or unknown to the
author, and all incidents are pure invention.

The Harlequin trademarks, consisting of the words
HARLEQUIN AMERICAN ROMANCE, HARLEQUIN
AMERICAN ROMANCES, and the portrayal of a Harlequin,
are trademarks of Harlequin Enterprises Limited; the portrayal
of a Harlequin is registered in the United States Patent and
Trademark Office and in the Canada Trade Marks Office.

Printed in Canada

Chapter One

Five minutes into Le Club, Terry was afraid she'd blown it.

It was six in the evening, the time when the club was the most crowded with the men and women converging on it from offices all over Manhattan. She had taken the elevator down to the women's locker room, walked to the end before finding an empty locker, and then looked around at the other women dressing and undressing. That was when she realized her shorts and tank top were not going to fit in.

Terry was supposed to blend in; instead, she stood out like a llama in a flock of sheep.

The outfits she saw around her were astounding. The one on the woman next to her exemplified the rest: a pink leotard was complemented by aqua tights over which pink-striped leg warmers—*in June?* Terry thought—hit the tops of aqua running shoes. Gold chains and diamond stud earrings, to say nothing of a perfectly made-up face and an exquisitely casual hairdo, topped it off. Terry began to wonder if she was in a health club or a disco.

She told herself that turning around and walking out would be just as conspicuous as getting into her workout clothes, but she wasn't convinced. Nevertheless, she stripped down and dressed in her personal version of exercise clothes. Then she sat down to put on thick cotton socks and well-worn sneakers. She was already figuring out where she would go to buy new workout clothes the next day when the thought hit her that that would be too obvious.

Anyway, Terry knew something about class. The kind of clothes being worn all around her were the kind worn by the upwardly mobile, the yuppies who had taken over half the city. People who were really rich didn't care how they looked—and since her cover was that she was rich, why worry about it?

She was getting looks from the other women in the locker room. Some, in fact, were staring at her outright. Terry affected a nonchalance she wasn't feeling and stared right back. She counted at least half a dozen who could have been runners-up in a Christie Brinkley look-alike contest. Then she decided that rich people wouldn't condescend to stare at the bourgeoisie, so she swept by them and headed for the elevators to take her up to the workout room.

The lobby of the building, which had reminded her of a luxury hotel, and even the well-equipped locker room, hadn't prepared Terry for the fourth floor. She was used to an occasional workout with free weights at the YMCA. After this, she might never be satisfied with the Y or free weights again.

She had never used Nautilus equipment before and she hadn't known how many different machines there were. Nor had she known there was a carpeted, creatively lit indoor track in the city, particularly one with wraparound lights and piped-in music. In addition, she was surrounded by the most beautiful specimens of manhood and womanhood she had ever seen outside of a Broadway musical.

Terry took her program card over to the instructors' desk. As a new member she would be given a program and shown how to use the various machines.

One of the instructors, a gorgeous young man who would have gotten her vote for a centerfold anytime, asked her if she knew how to use a stationary bicycle. When she said of course, he pointed her in the right direction and then said, "Warm up for twenty minutes on one of the bikes. Then I'll show you around."

Even the bikes turned out to be prepossessing. Something that looked like a gigantic digital watch was attached to the handlebars. It was flashing a message for her, something about putting in her program, as she seated herself on the bike. Since she didn't know the secret password, she ignored it.

After what seemed like twenty minutes she looked at her own digital watch and found that only two minutes had elapsed. That came as a shock, since her calves were already sore and her rear end was positively numb.

She hadn't been paying attention to anything but her own exhaustion but there seemed to be a sudden silence around her, then, an instant later, a distinct buzz of excitement. Terry looked around, and it appeared that the man now taking his place on the cycle next to hers was the cause of it.

She had heard that famous actors and models and such were members, but he didn't look familiar to her at all. Not that she'd recognize a model, but she did watch enough television and go to the movies often enough to know who was who in the entertainment world. Nor was he any famous rock star she had seen on MTV.

Although he was not familiar to her, Terry could acknowledge his good looks. If she had seen him on a subway, she probably would have stared at him. At Le Club, however, all the men were good-looking and the instructors were positively gorgeous. She was curious as to why this particular man was receiving all this attention. He had well-styled russet-colored hair, but it in no way compared with the instructor's head of curls, the color of old gold. The newcomer had a straight nose and high cheekbones and eyes that turned slightly downward, giving them an almost imperceptible Oriental cast. The instructor, on the other hand, looked as if he had modeled for Michelangelo in a former life. And while her neighbor's body was nicely proportioned, he was no Mr. Universe. She wouldn't pick him for a centerfold; he was more the type to be found in a cigarette ad—a sophisticated cigarette ad, not the Marlboro kind. In short, Terry couldn't see what all the fuss was about.

Young women who only moments before had been shunning the bikes were now competing for the one next to the mystery man, and Terry found herself being glared at by those who had missed out. She would gladly have given over her bike to any one of them except that she felt she had to go through with the twenty minutes in deference to her cover.

Despite the air-conditioning and the sweatband she wore, sweat was beginning to drip off her hair and into her eyes. She slowed down for a moment, and the man beside her said, "You have to do this." Then he punched several buttons on her bike's digital thing and lights flashed and the bike was suddenly harder to pedal. The clock on it now told her she had a full twenty minutes to go.

"Thanks a lot," Terry said, her sarcasm coming to the fore.

"You're just wasting your time if you don't do it right," he advised her, advice she could have lived without.

The woman on the other side of him, who was dressed in varying shades of violet, was now looking Terry over in much the same way tourists regard New York bag ladies who sleep in doorways. Terry ignored her and tried to look rich and indifferent, but she knew that all she really looked like was tired and sweaty.

"Your first time here?" Mr. Wonderful asked her, not even winded, even though he was pedaling four times faster than she was.

"Umm," Terry said, feeling too out of breath to speak.

"At least you dressed for it. Most of the women here dress to attract attention, not to work out."

Terry could take that as a compliment or infer that she wouldn't attract any attention. Since she knew what he was saying had the ear of every lovely young thing surrounding them—and she had to admit she was tired of their amused looks and the perfectly bonded smiles they aimed at her—she said, "I think clothes are a waste of money. I'll take a good investment any day." Terry was convinced that was how the rich talked.

For some reason, the response was a shocked silence from the women and a strangled laugh from Mr. Wonderful. Terry was waiting to hear what he'd have to say in reply, but there was only silence. When she finally looked over at his bike, he had already departed, and the woman who had been on his other side was now climbing onto the vacated cycle next to Terry.

"I like your reverse psychology," she said to Terry.

"I don't know what you're talking about."

"That remark about clothes. Maybe you're right—maybe that's the way to get to him. But I doubt it."

"I wasn't trying to get to him," Terry told her.

"Of course you weren't," the cyclist said in a very snotty tone of voice.

"What's the big deal? He doesn't look any better than any of the other men around. Anyway, I'm here to work out, not meet men."

"Of course. We all are. But still, it's not every day one gets to work out alongside Wynn Ransome."

"Who?" Terry gave up all pretense of pedaling.

The woman gave Terry a look of incredulity. "You really don't know who he is?"

Terry shook her head.

"Where've you been your whole life? In a cloister?"

Terry could only conclude that he was in some new TV show she hadn't yet seen, probably one of those nightly soaps she avoided. She waited to be clued in, but instead, the woman got off the bike and was immediately surrounded by a group of rainbow-hued young lovelies, most of whom were listening to her and looking at Terry.

"Wynn Ransome," Terry repeated to herself a few times, determined to remember the name long enough to find out who he was. She resumed pedaling, but then her bike made a noise and the digital lights went off, and she realized her time was up and she could now get down to the more serious stuff.

And about time. Much longer and she didn't think she would have been able to walk.

IN THE PAST TWO MONTHS three professional women in Terry's precinct had been murdered. The MO was the same on each. The killer had evidently either entered the apartments with the victims or at the victims' invitation, as there was no sign of forced entry. There was also evidence that the encounters had been social at first, a theory attested to by two wineglasses on the coffee tables of two of the victims and coffee cups, still half filled, in the apartment of the third. The victims were all the same type: medium height, slim and blond. The women had been strangled with their own long hair.

Terry wasn't assigned to the case but she had been following it. Anyone out to murder women was someone she was very interested in seeing apprehended. She was reading over the paperwork on the case one day when she had a few extra minutes, and she was the first one to catch a possible connection: all three victims had membership cards to Le Club in their wallets.

For a few seconds she fantasized about joining Le Club on her own and solving the case single-handedly. Then her more professional side took over and she went to Lieutenant Corbet's office and requested permission to speak to him.

The lieutenant was sitting with his perfectly polished shoes up on the desk, reading a report. Steve Corbet was six two, black, and a nearly perfect specimen of manhood. The only reason Terry qualified his perfection was because she had only seen him fully clothed. Who knew what imperfections might lurk beneath his three-piece suit? He was also a damn good cop.

"Come on in, Terry," he said, removing his feet from the desk and waving her to a chair. "How's the Simonton investigation coming along?"

The Simonton brothers, Nate and Al, had been gunned down in their collection agency. While it was difficult to find a suspect in most murder cases, in the case of the Simonton brothers just about anyone they had come into contact with had a motive. Jubilation at their deaths had been the order of the day whenever Terry had questioned a possible suspect. In other words, the investigation was going nowhere, and she told the lieutenant so. "It's this other thing," she said, "the women being killed."

"What's on your mind?"

She told him the connection she had found and he looked interested. "Yeah, I heard about that place. Biggest singles meeting spot on the East Side these days. I'd join myself if I could afford it." The lieutenant considered himself a ladies' man, and not without cause.

Terry said, "The problem is, the membership is probably in the thousands."

"Yeah, a little hard to check them all out."

They tossed it back and forth a little more; then Terry had to go out on one of her own leads. She forgot about it until the next day, when the lieutenant called her into his office first thing.

"You ever done decoy work, Terry?" he asked without any preliminaries.

"Before I got on homicide I did park detail for a while," she replied. That had involved lurking in Central Park and waiting to be mugged—not her all-time favorite duty.

"I was thinking about getting you into Le Club. It would have to be under cover, of course. If the killer is from there, it could be anyone. Mind being set up as a decoy?"

"Just one problem," she told him, although she could think of several. "I'm not a blonde."

He shrugged. "Not an insurmountable obstacle."

"A wig? It won't work. I can't work out and do the sauna and all that in a wig. Anyway the best wigs in the world look phony."

"Not willing to bleach your hair in the line of duty, huh?" Lieutenant Corbet challenged her with his eyes.

"Bleach doesn't make a blonde, sir. I'm Italian. I don't have the coloring for it. I'd end up looking like a cheap hooker and they'd throw me out of the place. Anyway all three of those women were lookers."

"You saying you don't get looks from the men on the squad?"

"Hell, Lieutenant, they'll look at anything."

That got a chuckle out of him. "Tell you what, Terry—you and me are going to have lunch together today."

"Yes, sir." And that was that. You didn't argue with the boss over everything.

As a matter of fact, Terry didn't even get lunch. The word "lunch" turned out to be a euphemism for being dragged into a wig store to try on their wares. Right away the lieutenant found a long, platinum-blond wig and thrust it at her with the order to try it on.

She did, and laughed out loud. "It's not going to work," she told him, noticing that even the eager saleswoman was trying not to laugh.

He was standing there inspecting her. "I've seen brown-eyed blondes before," he said.

"With dark eyebrows and skin?"

"You can lighten the eyebrows, can't you? As for the skin, it makes you look tan. I'll bet most of the people over there have tans. If not from the Hamptons, then from those tanning salons everyone's going to these days."

"I'm probably not his type even if I bleach my hair."

"It's worth a try, Terry."

She didn't have a choice anyway. He was right; it was worth a try, and she was the only female on the squad. And face it, she told herself, membership at Le Club, even if it was going to be work, wasn't something to turn down lightly. And for damn sure she wanted to catch the killer.

When they got back to the office Lieutenant Corbet called in Vince Moroni and Chris Kyle, the two detectives in charge of the case. He told them that he was switching Moroni to the Simonton case and putting Terry on with Kyle. Kyle was also going under cover at the health club as Terry's backup. The lieutenant didn't spell it out, but it was obvious why he chose Kyle rather than Moroni. Vince was a sharp cop, but at forty pounds overweight he'd be a sad specimen to send to Le Club.

Kyle was perfect. He looked more like a bodybuilder than a cop and had about the same amount of brains. He was also a major pain in the neck, always coming on to Terry in the office. Up until then she had managed to avoid working a case with him.

They discussed the case for a while. It was decided that Chris Kyle was to join Le Club that night and Terry would join him there in a few days, when her cover had been set up.

That was why, on the following Wednesday evening, instead of being in rush-hour traffic headed for Brooklyn, Terry was instead being shown the ropes—or in this case the machines—in a health club whose membership fees staggered the imagination, by a young man whose body measurements were equally staggering.

With a dazzling smile in place, he had said, "I'm Scott," and then led her over to what looked like a beautifully padded torture chamber, which turned out to be a machine to develop her pectoral muscles. The pectoral muscles being on the chest, this machine was something she figured she could use.

"What I want you to do...Terry," he said, after glancing down at her card to ascertain her name, "is start out on each machine at the lowest weight and do eight to twelve repetitions. As soon as you can do twelve reps, even if it's a strain, you immediately move to the next highest weight. Got it?"

"Yeah," she said, "but how do I work this machine?"

By the time she had finished the fourth machine on the circuit she was dripping wet but elated. The machines were half the work of the free weights and supposedly gave faster results. Her elation subsided when a look around told her she was the only female there who was sweating. And yet, to look at them, they were all using the machines just as she was. She had to conclude that in her case it was ninety percent nerves because of being under cover. At least she hoped that was the reason.

After completing the entire circuit, she decided to call it a night. There were free weights and whirlpools and saunas and a lot of other things, but she decided it was better to ease into it, and besides, she wasn't sure at that point whether she'd even make it home. Her legs were functioning, but just barely.

She had spotted Kyle a few times and it looked as if he was more interested in chatting with women than working out, which was the normal method of operation for him. Terry circled him, giving him the signal that she was leaving—and leaving alone—and saw his answering sign.

She was heading for the elevators when she spotted Wynn Ransome on some contraption that looked like a short escalator. He was walking up the stairs and getting nowhere, and she paused to watch.

He saw her standing there and said, "How'd it go?"

"I love the machines," she said.

"You ought to give this one a try."

"All it looks like is walking up stairs."

He was nodding. "Yes, but that's something most of us never do. It'll work some muscles you don't ordinarily use."

Terry was about to tell him that, on the contrary, she spent half her day walking up and down stairs on the job, but then she remembered she was supposed to be a rich playgirl and shut up. "Maybe next time," she told him.

A couple of guys in the elevator gave her looks, but she ignored them the way she was accustomed to ignoring the male cops at the station. Then it occurred to her that the way to attract a potential killer wasn't by being rude or by ignoring all the men around her. So just before she got off the elevator she smiled at one of them, but the only effect it produced was that he looked the other way.

Terry could see why once she hit the shower room and saw herself in the full-length mirror. She weighed 112 pounds soaking wet, and at that moment she might have weighed in at ten pounds more. An appetizing sight she was not. Also, catching sight of herself as a blonde continued to astonish her.

Terry had a theory that being a blonde was a state of mind. Never having been one, never even having aspired to being one, she didn't seem to have that requisite state of mind. In a nutshell, she just felt dumb.

Maybe if she had short blond hair it would have been easier. But what had once been her dark brown hair, which she wore in a long braid twisted into a bun for work and just kept in a long braid after hours, was now hanging loose and blond, held in place at the moment by a sweatband that hadn't performed its function and made her look like one of those princesses in the fairy tales who escape from the tower by letting down their hair.

The color wasn't so bad. In fact the hairdresser had done a fine job. Instead of giving her just long platinum hair, which was what she suspected the lieutenant had in mind, he had done it in varying shades from sandy-colored to the palest hue, making it look much more natural than one color would have looked. Her eyebrows had been lightened a couple of shades and, believe it or not, with her olive skin it did make her look as if she spent her days at the beach.

Terry showered and dressed, then handed in her towel and the key to her locker at the desk. The woman in charge said to her, "We prefer the members not wear street clothes to work out."

"I didn't," Terry told her. "I wore shorts and a top."

"We prefer leotards and tights."

Terry couldn't believe it. "You mean I've got to dress like some ballerina?"

"It's not a matter of aesthetics," she was told, although Terry doubted the woman meant it. "We find it's more sanitary. That way the members don't leave perspiration on the machines."

Remembering the tons of sweat she had left on every single machine, Terry felt embarrassed. Then she also remembered that all the men had been wearing shorts, and some of them must have sweat. She pointed that out to the woman, using her newly acquired rich-bitch voice, and the woman instantly backed down, suggesting that Terry carry a towel around with her to wipe off the machines after she used them.

That was a compromise Terry could live with.

She headed on foot to the sublet the lieutenant had found for her on East Fifty-third Street, one of the more expensive neighborhoods in a city where cheap neighborhoods were now nonexistent.

Over the past weekend Terry had explained to her family that she was going to have to live in the city during the week for the duration of the case. Her father had seemed a bit put out, which wasn't like him, because he generally liked having Mike around. Her son didn't seem to care one way or another. In fact, he was probably trying to hide his glee; his grandfather let him get away with murder when Terry wasn't there to provide some discipline.

On Monday, Terry had spent hours in an expensive salon having her hair done, and also having something done with her nails while she was at it. On Monday evening the lieutenant took her over to what was going to be her home away from home for a while. The building was a small, expensive residential hotel with a doorman, a concierge and other luxuries she wasn't accustomed to. Her own apartment, though, came as a surprise. It had its own private entrance on the street, which meant the killer could just knock on her door without having to get past a doorman, an eventuality she pointed out to Lieutenant Corbet.

"But that's the beauty of it, Terry," he said to her, putting a key into the lock and ushering her inside.

Terry failed to see the beauty and told him so.

"But a doorman might put him off, and we wouldn't like that, would we?"

She gave a noncommittal grunt.

He went around turning on concealed lighting and she found herself looking at a large living room done in gray and pink, neither of which color she liked. The furniture was all soft curves and looked as if it were made of plastic.

"Exquisite, isn't it?" asked the lieutenant, and Terry did a double take to see if he was kidding. He wasn't.

"I've never seen furniture like this," she said.

"Art deco, the latest thing."

At least there was a stereo and a TV, although both were cunningly hidden away in curvy gray cabinets.

"Wait until you see the bathroom," he said, leading her through a bedroom that was done in the same colors as the living room.

The bathroom had the usual things plus a bidet, something Terry had never actually seen before, and a sunken tub that could have held a group. She felt embarrassed just looking at it.

"What do you think?" Lieutenant Corbet asked her.

"Pretty impressive."

"You bet it is. But you haven't seen the best yet."

She thought he was referring to the kitchen, but he walked right through that particular room and opened a door that led out to a garden. A used-brick patio with white wrought-iron furniture was shaded by trees, and he was right, it was the best part.

"This is really nice," she told him, finally sounding enthusiastic.

"Bet you never thought you'd be living in luxury as a police officer, did you?"

She shook her head. No, she never had thought so, particularly since she wasn't into taking bribes.

As they passed back through the kitchen, she gave it a cursory look, which was all it deserved. Whoever's apartment it was certainly never cooked. Not a pot or pan in sight; it was as barren and immaculate as a kitchen in a model home.

The lieutenant made himself at home on the curved chaise in the bedroom and discussed her cover as she hung her few clothes in the closet.

"Are you listening to me?" he asked at one point.

"I'm listening."

"What did I say?"

"You said I'm independently wealthy but I will occasionally do interior decorating for fun. Which is a laugh; I didn't even know what this furniture was called."

"It shouldn't come up in conversation anyway. Someone out to kill you isn't going to ask your advice on decorating. The wealthy part, though... Are those all the clothes you've got, Terry?"

She looked at the closet, now a quarter filled with her clothes. "It's all I packed. These should last for a while."

The lieutenant gave what could only be considered a discreet cough. "I think we better do some shopping tomorrow, Terry."

"Are you saying there's something wrong with my clothes?"

"Not at all. They're perfect for your job, your way of life. They're just not right for the part you're portraying."

"I've got clothes to work out in."

"Yes, but you'll be going to and from Le Club. And you'll no doubt be seen at those times."

"I don't need any more clothes," she protested.

"The department will pay for them—they won't cost you a cent."

But on that point Terry was adamant, and the lieutenant finally backed down, hoping, she was sure, that she'd never be seen outside of Le Club.

Her first night in the apartment had seemed strange to Terry, and the second one wasn't any better. The thing was, it was the first time in her thirty-three years she had ever lived alone. She had lived at home up until she was twenty; then she had married Nick and lived with him. And when he died, she had her son to live with. At times she had wondered what it would be like to live alone, but this was even worse than she had imagined.

Terry took care of the quiet by keeping the TV on when she was home, but it still wasn't noisy enough. She guessed it was the constant ringing of the phone she missed. At least once a day she was used to hearing from her grandmother or her aunts or her brother and sister and their respective spouses. For some reason, every time someone in her family needed advice, they called on her. Terry thought it had something to do with the fact that she was a cop. They seemed to think this meant she knew everything.

Everyone but her son, that is. Mike didn't think she knew anything, but then Terry had been the same way at his age.

Her father, for some reason, was being unusually silent of late. Generally she'd have to listen to everything he had been doing, but lately he'd become secretive. Terry assumed it was a new girlfriend, although he usually told her about them. At fifty-four, looking like an aging Bruce Springsteen who had kept in shape, her dad had no trouble finding women. In fact, they usually found him. Ever since her mom died, Terry had kept waiting for him to get remarried, but as time went by he seemed to have settled pretty well into living alone.

Terry wasn't supposed to give out her new phone number to her relatives, just to her father and Mike in case of an emergency, but by Wednesday night, after her first session at Le Club, she felt in dire need of some familiar conversation.

That was how she found out who Wynn Ransome was. Her father hadn't known, nor had her son, but when she called her sister, Kathy knew right away.

"What about him?" Kathy wanted to know.

"Nothing. I was just wondering who he was."

Kathy sighed. "He designs sport clothes. You must have seen them around, Terry. Everyone's wearing them. They have 'WIN' written on them."

"Is that how he spells his name? W-I-N?"

"No, W-Y-N-N. Why are you asking about him, anyway?"

"He belongs to the same health club I belong to."

"You mean Wynn Ransome goes to the Y?"

"No, Kathy. I told you about it over the weekend, only you weren't listening. So what's new with you?"

What was new with Kathy took her a full hour to relate, and what it amounted to was that Kathy thought her husband was fooling around on her and wanted Terry to follow him and find out.

"Why don't you just ask him?" Terry suggested, refusing to take it seriously.

"And have him lie to me?"

"I can't follow him for you, Kath. I'm on a job. Anyway, I wouldn't go around following Johnny."

"Why not? You follow criminals, don't you?"

"No. And anyway, Johnny's no criminal."

There was a long silence, then, "My own sister and you won't even help."

"If you want him followed, Kathy, follow him yourself."

"Maybe I will."

"Or better yet, talk to him."

Nothing was resolved by the time Terry got off the phone, except that her sister was now mad at her. But Terry knew she'd be over it by the next night.

As she got ready for bed she tried to remember if she'd seen any clothes around with WIN printed on them. She didn't think so, but then she seldom noticed clothes.

What the woman at Le Club had said to her about using reverse psychology now made sense, and Terry chuckled at what Wynn Ransome must have thought when she told him she thought clothes were a waste of money.

Well, she still thought they were and, what's more, she thought spending his life designing clothes had to be a great big waste of time.

And then she stopped thinking about clothes and Wynn Ransome and got back to thinking about the case she was on. But it did cross her mind that a clothes designer would be an unlikely suspect. Unless maybe he was killing off women who didn't wear his designs.

That was so ridiculous it made her laugh out loud. But after she finished laughing, she did begin to think about motive. If she could figure out why the killer was killing, she'd be almost there.

Unfortunately, no motive came to mind.

FOR THE LIFE OF HIM, Wynn couldn't figure out why he had spoken to her. Unless maybe it was because she was the only female within shouting distance who wasn't trying—and not always subtly—to get his attention.

Women recognizing him and coming on to him were becoming a real nuisance. Not that he didn't like women, but the kind of women who were attracted to him were the kind whose sole interest in life was clothes. For some reason they thought he'd want to "talk clothes" with them, which was virtually the last thing he felt like talking about when he wasn't actually at work.

He knew that if he hadn't been in Le Club he wouldn't have even noticed her. But since she was there she stuck out. In fact, the only thing "Le Club" about her was her hair and, paradoxically, that was the only thing about her that didn't seem to fit.

For one thing, her clothes were all wrong. All wrong for Le Club, that was. For mowing the lawn in Westchester they'd probably be just the thing. For him they were just the thing. In fact, she was dressed almost exactly like him, only his shorts and tank top were in better shape and his sneakers hadn't been bought at the local Woolworth's, or whoever put out that hideous model. It was just that at Le Club the women dressed quite differently from the men, not because it made any sense and not even because dance gear was the best thing to wear when exercising. His personal opinion was that such clothing was worn because it was flattering and for no other reason.

When he took the cycle beside hers, his first impression of her was that she had too much blond hair and she was dressed like a boy. All this was strange enough at Le Club, but then he noticed that she hadn't put a program into the computer on the bike. That didn't make any sense at all unless she was new and the instructors had been too busy to see that she did it right.

He didn't say anything for a while, but finally it began to annoy him that she was wasting her time—and her money—and getting nothing in return. But when he adjusted the bike for her, all she'd done was glare at him. And that glare rather shocked him, because she had the darkest eyes he'd ever seen, so dark he couldn't even discern the pupils in them.

Then, because he was getting annoyed at all the other women hovering around, watching him, listening to anything he might have to say, he decided to compliment her on the way she was dressed, because he was sure she had been embarrassed when she had shown up and seen she was dressed all wrong. And the only thanks he got was her smart remark about clothes being a waste of money.

To think he had actually believed at that point that she hadn't known who he was. He should've known there wouldn't be anyone at the clothes-conscious health club who didn't know who he was.

He was, however, wrong. Later, when he was on the abdominal machine, he overheard two women talking about what had been said between him and Blondie on the exercycles. He realized she really hadn't recognized him—which shouldn't have surprised him too much because she didn't look as if she knew the first thing about clothes.

That thought gave him pause. Had he really become the sort of person who judged others by their clothes?

He was afraid the answer was yes. But his work revolved around clothes and it was hard not to be oriented in that direction. Still, he was ashamed enough of himself to be pleasant to her when he saw her for a second time, which, again, didn't go unnoticed. But the hell with it. So Wynn Ransome himself was seen talking to the candidate for "worst dressed" at Le Club. So what?

It wasn't going to make the front page of the *Times*, that was for sure.

On the other hand, there was *WWD*.

Chapter Two

Terry spent Thursday and Friday doing some investigating on her own. Morini and Kyle had compiled comprehensive reports that gave her all the facts, but when she worked on a case she liked to do it her way. She had found in the past that she often noticed things the men overlooked.

If she was being set up as a decoy, she wanted to know everything possible about what she was going up against. She also wanted to see for herself if she was similar enough to the victims to make the murderer pick her out of the crowd at Le Club.

The only apartment that was still available for Terry to see was that of the latest victim, Ann Shelby, who had been, at age thirty, a vice-president of a Wall Street brokerage firm. Her death had occurred only days before, and the department still had her apartment under wraps.

Terry told Kyle she wanted to take a look at it and he insisted on going along. He gave her his crude grin, which was meant to convey that he thought she was trying to get him alone in an empty apartment. She ignored it, which wasn't a difficult thing to do. She was used to ignoring Chris Kyle. If she didn't ignore him, she was afraid she'd give in to an overwhelming urge to kick him in the rear end.

Never letting up on his machismo for a moment, Kyle insisted on doing the driving, even though the car was signed out to Terry. While driving he kept up a running commentary on all the "broads" he had met at Le Club. To hear him talk, he could have had any one of them if he'd felt like it—which was a bold-faced lie, because Kyle always felt like it.

Terry finally tuned him out and concentrated instead on trying to get the car's air-conditioner to work, which was a losing proposition. It was only the beginning of June but consistently high temperatures were already breaking records and worsening the drought.

Ann Shelby had lived in a co-op on East Sixty-seventh Street. It turned out to be a small one-bedroom apartment, but Terry knew what those kinds of places went for. She decided that Shelby had to have been making a big salary.

Terry talked Kyle into getting something to eat while she looked around alone, and, surprisingly, he didn't give her a hard time. That was unusual for him, so she deduced he must be hungry.

Except for all the travel books on the shelves in the living room, there was nothing of interest in that room. Terry briefly looked into the kitchen, which appeared to have been used about as frequently as the one in her own sublet and made her wonder if it was only in Brooklyn that women still cooked.

She had only seen pictures of Shelby dead, but she still recognized her in the silver-framed photos on the dresser in the victim's bedroom. In most of them she appeared with different men; in two she was alone. In all of them she looked lovely. Other than the fact that they both had blond hair, Terry didn't see any resemblance between the victim and herself.

Ann Shelby had had very widely spaced blue eyes, delicate features and the slim body of an athlete, which wasn't surprising, since in three of the pictures she appeared with a tennis racket, and Terry knew that she had belonged to Le Club for the past two years. Terry finally got depressed looking at Shelby's perfect body and decided to take a look in the closet.

One side of the double-width closet was filled with garments suitable for the victim's executive status; the other side held sport clothes. Terry lifted a few tops out by the hangers and was surprised, although she shouldn't have been, to see WIN printed on each of them—once on a pocket, twice just above the hem and one time in large letters diagonally across the chest.

Terry immediately jumped to the stupid conclusion that Wynn Ransome plied his lady friends with clothes and then murdered them. Terry knew that was not the kind of deductive reasoning a good police detective used. Anyway, judging by the reactions of the women at Le Club, Wynn didn't need to force his attentions on anyone.

Terry put the clothes back and couldn't help but note the king-size bed that dwarfed the room. It could, of course, just mean that Shelby liked a lot of room in which to sleep. It could also mean she liked company sleeping over. That, she reminded herself, was none of her concern, or business.

Terry left the apartment. She found Kyle eating a hot dog from a street vendor and decided to join him.

"Satisfy your curiosity?" Kyle asked her.

"You brought in her address book, didn't you?"

He had just shoved the rest of the hot dog into his mouth, so he only nodded in reply.

"I want to take a look at it, maybe talk to some of her friends."

"They've already been questioned. Also her boyfriends."

Shelby's boyfriends didn't interest Terry, but she wanted to get more of a personal feel for the victim and she thought she could get that from friends—if Shelby was the type of woman to have female friends.

That evening Terry made a few phone calls to some of the names in Shelby's address book. Most of the women were willing to answer her casual questions and all professed a desire to have the killer apprehended.

One thing one of the women said interested Terry. She told Terry that Ann Shelby was the type who would die rather than make a scene.

"You mean that literally?" Terry asked.

"No, not really. But close to it. If she knew the killer, she'd let him in because it was the polite thing to do."

"And if she didn't know him?"

"No, that would be different. We're all a little paranoid about living in New York."

Terry wondered about that later. She knew how she'd react if some guy tried to force his way into her apartment, or even talk his way in. Making a scene wouldn't daunt her in the least; she'd scream bloody hell. But she was a New Yorker, born and bred, and perhaps it was different for women who came from small towns, places where one was expected to be neighborly and friendly and where no one took advantage of this.

On Friday night Terry drove to Le Club, since she would be heading home to Brooklyn afterward. She found a parking space easily, and when she got inside she saw that the place wasn't nearly as crowded as it had been on Wednesday night. She asked one of the women in the locker room about it and was told it was because many of the offices in the city closed early on Friday in the summer, and everyone headed right out for the Hamptons.

That was news to Terry. She didn't know anyone who headed out for the Hamptons on Friday afternoons. Maybe Coney Island on Saturdays, but that was about it.

Her instructor, Scott, greeted her like an old friend and asked if she had been sore after her workout.

"A little," she admitted—a gross understatement, to say the least.

"Did you try the whirlpool afterward?"

She shook her head. "I was too tired."

"Best thing in the world for sore muscles. Did you bring a swimsuit along?"

She said she hadn't.

"Well, next time bring it. You could work a little swimming in, too."

Terry figured she could work in a lot of things if she was willing to devote all her waking hours to her body, which she wasn't. He was just being helpful and friendly, though, so she thanked him and then headed over to the bicycles.

This time Wynn Ransome wasn't seated next to her, but the woman who had asked her if she'd spent her whole life in a cloister was. Terry was surprised she even recognized the woman, as she had exchanged her ballerina outfit for shorts and a tank top. They weren't as worn as Terry's, but they weren't anything special, either.

Terry nodded to her and the woman said hi.

"Did you find out who Wynn Ransome is?" she asked Terry.

"Yeah. My sister told me. I'm really not into clothes."

"I thought that was just a ploy to get him interested."

"No, he's all yours," Terry told her.

The woman looked down at herself in a deprecating way and said, "I decided to go for comfort, too. Particularly since they're not allowed to air-condition the building all that much because of the drought."

The excuse made sense, but Terry didn't believe her. She figured the woman just wanted to hear Wynn compliment her on her practical attire.

The woman said, "I'm Lisa." Terry introduced herself and then she had to stop talking altogether in the interests of being able to breathe.

She had realized, though, that Lisa wasn't being snotty that night, or maybe she had been wrong about her the first time. She also recognized the fact that Lisa had long, blond hair, and she decided she'd keep an eye on her. But then, looking around, Terry saw that it would be impossible to keep an eye on all the long-haired blondes; they were everywhere.

Anyway, from what she could see, Kyle was single-handedly taking on that task.

She got a good workout on the machines and even put in some time with the free weights. She hadn't seen Wynn Ransome around and figured he was one of the lemmings converging on the Hamptons. But when she got in the elevator, he was standing alone in the back, dressed only a brief swimsuit, with his wet hair slicked back.

He nodded to her and said, "How's it going?"

Making a concerted effort not to stare at his half-naked body, Terry was trying to remember why she had thought he wasn't the centerfold type. "Okay," she mumbled.

"Have you used the pool yet?"

She shook her head, quickly averting her eyes once again.

"You ought to give it a try. Swimming's probably the most perfect exercise there is."

Terry believed him, if his body was any indication. "Then why waste time on the machines?" she asked, this time meeting his eyes and deciding they were a safer part of his body to stare at.

He gave a slow smile, now looking like a combination centerfold/cigarette ad. This close, he really was devastating.

"It's all the exercise I get," he said.

She was thinking of his clothes or, rather, the clothes he designed, in Ann Shelby's apartment, but for the life of her she couldn't summon up any fear of him. At that moment, if he were to reach out for her, she would not believe it would be with the intention of strangling her.

She belatedly realized that the elevator had come to her stop, and she said, "Well, see you around," which was the most scintillating remark she could come up with.

She was showering when Lisa showed up. "I saw you get into the elevator with Wynn Ransome," Lisa said, "but I couldn't get to it before the door closed."

"If you had yelled, I would've held it for you."

She gave Terry a suspicious look, as though wondering if Terry were being sarcastic, but then decided she wasn't. "I wouldn't have wanted to make a scene."

That line sounded familiar. "Why not?" Terry asked her, really wanting to know. It wouldn't have bothered her at all to yell for someone to hold an elevator.

"Why wouldn't I want to make a scene?"

Terry nodded.

"Men don't like it."

"If it hadn't been Wynn would you have cared?"

"I guess so. I suppose I haven't been in New York long enough to get that assertive."

Terry would have to give some thought to that. Maybe New Yorkers were assertive, but then again, maybe they had to be in order to survive.

Lisa said, "What'd he have to say? Anything?"

"He'd been swimming. Told me it was the perfect exercise."

Lisa's eyes widened. "Was he in a swimsuit?"

"I think so." As if she hadn't been trying not to stare at his body the entire time.

"How'd he look?"

Terry's innate honesty came to the fore. "Spectacular."

Lisa gave her a genuine grin. "So you're not a nun after all."

"I never said I was a nun, Lisa. I just said I wasn't here to meet men."

"Then you've got to be the only one. This club has taken the place of singles bars, didn't you know that?"

"I never went to singles bars, either."

Lisa gave Terry a knowing look. "Oh, you're going with someone, is that it?"

Terry shook her head.

"I give up. What's your problem?"

At that point Terry would normally have told her that she had a son who took most of her free time, but since she was supposed to be a rich playgirl, she improvised. "Oh, I see men now and then, but I'm not ready to get serious."

Lisa looked her over as though maybe Terry was younger than she looked. Then, realizing she was staring at Terry's naked body, she blushed and turned away.

Terry decided to do a little investigating and said, "Do you get asked out much here?"

"Sometimes, but hardly ever by the right people."

"You mean not by someone you're attracted to?"

Lisa turned back to her. "Attraction hasn't got anything to do with it. It's just that you can't judge these guys by their looks, that's all. Some of the best-looking ones just scrape together the entrance fee in order to meet women with some bucks. I'm not really interested in some guy who makes less money than I do. I mean, an unemployed actor might look good, but you're left picking up the check."

That was interesting, but Terry didn't want to pursue it because the next logical question would be to ask what Lisa did, and that would lead to Lisa's asking Terry what she did, and that would lead to Terry's having to admit she did nothing. Which would be embarrassing, since Terry knew she actually worked—and worked hard—for a living. Instead, she left the shower and dried off.

She was dressed before Lisa and left, telling her she'd see her on Monday. Lisa really wasn't so bad, but Terry didn't feel she should strike up any friendships when everything she said would have to be a lie.

Terry lived in Mill Basin Marina, a section of Brooklyn so remote the subway didn't even go that far. That meant that if you worked in Manhattan, as she did, you had two possible methods of commuting: either a private bus service—but the problem with that was that the last bus left Manhattan at 6:30 P.M.—or a car. Terry chose the latter option.

She drove an old Willy's Jeep that was paid for and reliable. It was also open, so she got snowed on in the winter and alternately rained on and baked alive during the rest of the year. In other words, it was about as comfortable as where she lived.

When her building went condo a year back, she found that affordable apartments in the city no longer existed. Her father, who was retired and living on a boat in the marina, was moving into a larger boat and offered his old one, a thirty-foot cabin cruiser, rent-free.

"It'll save me the cost of putting it in dry dock for the winter," he told her, but she knew he was just trying to help out. He was always telling her she was too independent for her own good, which was no doubt true, but that time she took him up on his offer.

Originally she was only going to use the boat until she found an apartment, but it turned out to be so perfect she had no immediate plans to leave. The main reason it was so perfect was because of her son. Mike not only thought it was the greatest adventure in the world to live on a boat, but at twelve he also thought he was too old for a baby-sitter. With Pop living right next door to him, so to speak, Terry no longer worried about him when she wasn't there.

The only disadvantage to the boat was having Mike's dog living on it. Pop had brought home a puppy for Mike when they first moved onto the boat. Since they hadn't been allowed to have pets in the apartment, and since the marina had no such restrictions, she had said yes to the puppy.

Well, that puppy gradually grew to be the size of a small horse. He was sweet and friendly, and Terry loved Henry dearly, but every time he walked across the deck, the boat listed. If he got any bigger, she was afraid he'd sink them one night.

The drive home was long, but she made better time than usual since rush hour was over and the traffic had thinned out. She stopped at the supermarket near the marina for a few things, forgetting she was a blonde until a couple of the local wise guys started making suggestive remarks to her. She told them to knock it off, and they belatedly recognized her and managed looks of chagrin.

Even before she got to the marina she could hear Mike's music. Despite the fact that she had given him a Walkman for Christmas, he still insisted on blaring out his music on his old cassette player, so that every occupant of every boat was forced to listen to it whether they liked rock or not. Unfortunately, music really carried over water.

Walking down the dock, she could see that Pop's boat was dark, which surprised her. Usually Mike spent his time over there when she wasn't home.

She leaped onto her boat and went down the steps to the cabin. A pair of dark eyes looked at her in shock, and without her even asking, Mike turned off the music, which made Henry start barking for no reason at all.

She remembered that it was the first time Mike had seen her as a blonde. "Hey, it's part of the job," she told him, suddenly feeling foolish.

"This I gotta hear," said Mike, starting to grin. "Hey, you look sexy, Mom."

"Yeah, right," Terry muttered.

"I mean it. What made you do it, anyway?"

"That's a long story," she said, knowing he wouldn't give her any peace until she told him. So she launched into it, but halfway through Mike said, "That sounds pretty dangerous."

"Not really, because I know what I'm up against."

"You don't mind, do you?" he asked her.

"Mind what?"

"Being in danger."

He really seemed to want to know, so she said, "Sometimes I do. It's just that this one doesn't feel dangerous to me."

Mike seemed to think about that for a moment, then changed the subject. "What're we going to eat?"

"Didn't Grandpa feed you?"

"No, he's out on a date."

"Really? Who with?"

"He didn't say. He's not talking about this one for some reason."

So she hadn't been wrong. Mike was finding him secretive, too. "I don't like him leaving you alone," she said, then instantly regretted it when she saw the look of disgust on Mike's face.

"Come on, Mom. I'm twelve, you know. I don't need a baby-sitter. Most of the girls my age are baby-sitters themselves."

"Yeah, I know. Sorry I said that."

"As a matter of fact," he said, not meeting her eyes, "I'm going on a date tomorrow night."

That was a first, and Terry was pretty surprised. The last she had heard he hadn't even liked girls. "Really? Where are you going?"

He shrugged. "No big deal. Just to a movie at King's Plaza."

But it was his first date and she thought it was a big deal. "Who's the girl?"

"You don't know her. I met her around."

Since he went to a Catholic boys' school, she wondered what "around" meant. On the other hand, that was probably something the girl's parents should be more worried about than she, so she decided not to interrogate him any further, at least for the moment.

"Want to go out for a pizza?" she asked him.

"Yeah, great," he said, showing the kind of animation a twelve-year-old boy always shows toward junk food.

Terry had been looking forward all week to being home for the weekend with her father and Mike, and now Pop was out on a date, Mike was going out on a date, and she appeared to be the only one without any social life. It had never bothered her before, but suddenly it did.

Even a pepperoni pizza with everything on it didn't quite cheer her up.

THE NEXT MORNING, when Mike was off in the rowboat with his friends, Terry jumped across to Pop's deck to see what was up.

Surprisingly, Pop wasn't even up. When she saw that he was still asleep, she put on some coffee and decided to fix him breakfast.

By the time the sausage was sizzling he was out of bed and looking into the galley, his hair standing up straight on his head. "Morning, Terry," he said. "What's this in honor of?"

Not wanting to tell him he deserved it for all the times he had done it for her, which would have embarrassed him, she said, "It's in honor of the fact I want to use your shower." Unlike the one on her boat, his had real hot water.

"You're always welcome to use my shower."

"And I always appreciate it."

They were both being overly polite, which didn't bode well, since she wanted to question him on where he'd been the night before.

He was through with the meal before she got up her courage. Then she just blurted it out. "Where were you last night, Pop?"

"Keeping track of your old man now?"

She tried to mask her annoyance. "Just curious, that's all."

"Do I ask you where you go at night?"

"I don't go anywhere."

"Do I even ask you why you suddenly show up as a blonde?"

She had to laugh at that. "All right, Pop. I'll tell you why I'm blond if you tell me where you were last night." And with whom, she thought.

"You're getting worse than your sister." That was a real slur, because Kathy was the nosiest person in the world.

"Forget it," she told him. "I really don't care anyway."

"That's good, because it's none of your business."

All of which got the weekend off to a great start.

Her brother, Tony, who had been out of work for the past six months and was driving his wife, Joanna, crazy because he refused to let her get a job, dropped by with two of his kids. Tony was a younger version of Pop, and Terry had a soft spot for the brother she had helped raise when their mother died. So she listened to him and didn't criticize his thinking, although she knew what his problem was.

The youngest child, Tony had grown up always behind his older sisters in everything, and as a result he had become overly competitive. When he married Joanna, they had both been working, and that competitiveness carried over to her. He had been much happier when, after they got married, Joanna quit her job. Plus, he had Pop as an example, who, although proud of Terry, really believed women belonged at home.

Now, with his unemployment compensation at an end and their savings being eaten up, Joanna wanted to find a job until Tony found work. That's what Terry would have done in her shoes, but it was no good telling Tony that because what he was looking for was support.

Instead, she just listened and didn't offer any opinion at all. She only hoped he'd find work soon.

Then Kathy came over with all three of her kids, and Terry realized that at some point, while she had been listening to Tony, Pop had disappeared. She was about to mention his secretive behavior to the others when Kathy interrupted about Johnny, and then Mike came home and wanted to talk to her in private. They went over to their boat and the first thing he said was, "I'm not sure about this date."

"What aren't you sure about?"

"Maybe it's not such a good idea."

"You said it was just a movie. What's the big deal?"

He shrugged, suddenly looking younger than his twelve years. "I don't know what I'm supposed to wear."

She tried to think back to what she had worn on dates, and all she could come up with was jeans. "Just wear what you'd wear with the guys," she told him.

He gave her a mistrustful look. "On a date?"

"Why not? It's not like it's a dance or anything."

He still looked dubious. "I thought you were supposed to dress up for a date."

Maybe he was right, and she was going to send him off looking like a freak. "I think what's important, Mike, is that you feel comfortable. If you're in clothes you don't feel comfortable in, you're not going to be at ease with your date."

"I'm comfortable like this," he said, looking down at his cutoffs and bare feet.

"Then go like that," she said, hoping he wouldn't.

"I guess I'll wear some jeans," he finally said.

"And take a shower first," she advised.

His face looked betrayed. "What for? I've been swimming all day."

Terry decided that if it made him feel more comfortable to smell of salt water and fish, who was she to argue? It wasn't as if she were that familiar with the dating scene.

That night when her brother had gone home to his wife, Kathy had gone home to Johnny, Pop had again disappeared, and Mike had gone out on his first date, she began to feel very sorry for herself.

She found she was missing Nick more than she had in years. At times she could hardly remember what he looked like and had to get out old pictures of him, but she hadn't forgotten how it felt to be with him, to have him around. For one thing, she could discuss work with him, and that was something it was awfully hard to do with a civilian.

For another, he had been more than just her husband; he had been her childhood friend. They had grown up in the same apartment building, run around with the same gangs, and when she had gone to a Catholic girls' school, he had elected to go to the Catholic boys' high school only two blocks away from it, even though his parents would have allowed him to go to public school.

And in those days they all thought public school spelled freedom.

He had taken her out on her first date, given her her first kiss, and when he quit Brooklyn College after one year to join the police force, she had followed along. Being a cop hadn't been any ambition of hers, but she wanted to do whatever Nick did. That she took to it so well was just a bonus. But when Mike was born, she had gladly retired.

Mostly, though, she missed Nick at night. Once you got used to a warm body next to yours in bed at night, it was awfully hard to go back to cold sheets. She didn't mean sex; she meant comfort. Bed never seemed as comfortable as it had when Nick was around.

Of course, when Nick had been around they'd had a double bed. Now she slept in what was a breakfast nook by day and became two small, hard cots at night. But it had its compensations. No matter how hot it got in the city, there was always a breeze off the water at the marina, and the rocking of the boat usually lulled her to sleep.

Not tonight, though. Tonight the rocking of the boat was being caused more by Henry than by the water. Maybe it was because Mike wasn't home yet, but whatever the reason, Henry seemed to be lumbering from one side of the boat to the other. *Hurricane Henry,* she thought with amusement.

She heard Mike when he came in but decided to pretend she was asleep. Too well she remembered Pop's questioning after she'd been out on a date with Nick and she didn't want to put Mike through the same thing.

In the morning, though, she didn't even have to ask. The first thing Mike said to her when she returned from Mass was, "I don't think dating's so great."

"Movie no good?" she asked him.

"It was boring. She made me go see some love story."

"Well, maybe she finds science fiction movies boring."

"Mom, no one finds science fiction movies boring. Anyway, I paid for it—it should've been my choice."

"Well, I'm sorry you didn't have fun."

"What a waste. I could've been out with the guys."

All of which was rather a relief to Terry; she hadn't thought his dating life would begin so soon.

Still, he took off to go to twelve o'clock Mass with his friends, then on to a science fiction movie, and she was left with nothing to do but clean up the boat, a thankless task with a twelve-year-old around. To say nothing of a small horse.

When the phone rang, she literally jumped at it. Anything was better than the monotony of the day.

It was Kyle. "There's been another one, Terry," he said, sounding more serious than usual. "I figured you'd want to be in on it."

Trying to reconcile her excitement that something was happening with her horror that another woman had been killed, she told him that she'd be there as quickly as possible, then wrote down the address.

She didn't even change out of her jeans, just left a note for Mike and almost ran to her Jeep. An hour later she was trying to find a parking space on East Thirty-seventh Street.

She met Kyle in the hallway outside the victim's apartment. The lab boys and the medical examiner were already at work, but she went in to take a look around anyway. Kyle, for once showing some sensitivity, had told her she didn't have to view the body, but she wasn't feeling squeamish about it. After all, the killer didn't mutilate the women, and a strangled person wasn't the worst thing she'd ever had to look at.

Terry changed her mind when she saw the victim. Her long, blond hair was tied so tightly around her neck that it had cut her skin in places. Her face was swollen and her eyes were bulging.

"Looks like she's been dead a couple of days," someone was saying, and Terry turned away to get her stomach under control.

When she found Kyle having a smoke outside the building, she accepted his offer of a cigarette even though she rarely smoked. She thought it might lessen the feeling that her stomach was going to war with her intestines.

"What do you know about her?" Terry asked him.

"So far, just her name and the fact that she's a member of Le Club."

"How'd you find that out so fast?"

He grinned a superior grin. "Easy. I called Le Club and asked if she was a member. They're cooperating with us, you know."

"They must be worried about the publicity they're likely to get if this ever gets out."

"Yeah, but the publicity would be worse if it was found out they weren't cooperating."

"I don't know," Terry mused. "Maybe they ought to close the place down."

"For what? If they did that, Terry, the guy would just move elsewhere."

"Do you remember seeing her there, Kyle?"

"I don't think so. What about you?"

"I don't think so, either." She didn't add that many of the young women at Le Club looked just the same. At least when all dressed in the same kind of clothes.

"What we need to find out," she said, "is when she worked out last, and if anyone saw her with a guy."

"How're we going to do that without blowing our cover?"

"I don't know. I think maybe the lieutenant ought to give us more help, though. Someone ought to be over at Le Club right now while their memories are still warm."

Kyle nodded. "I could call Moroni. He wouldn't mind putting in the time. Since his wife left him, he doesn't have much to do on weekends."

Terry hadn't even known Moroni's wife had left him, but that was all right with her. She got enough gossip from her family; if she was being left out of office gossip, she considered that a plus.

Kyle called Moroni, who drove right in from Staten Island. He went directly to Le Club, and they waited for him in a coffee shop on Second Avenue.

Kyle managed to consume three hamburgers, and Terry had to sit by and watch, her stomach still queasy. When Moroni arrived, he shook his head before he even sat down.

"No go," he said. "No one remembers anything. They said that every female there talks to some male or another and it's not their job to keep track. They did come up with one thing. Another of their members, a Joy Freeman, brought her in as a new member. They said they thought the two of them were friends."

"Did you get her number?" Terry asked him.

"Yeah, but it's no dice. Her roommate said she wouldn't be back until late tonight."

"I guess there's nothing else we can do at the moment," said Kyle. "What do you say, Moroni, want to hit some of the local bars?" Looking over at Terry, he added, "You're welcome, too, of course," but he didn't sound eager for her to join them.

"No thanks," she said. She let them think she was heading home, but she wanted to get another look at the victim's apartment, maybe question the neighbors to see whether they had heard or seen anything. She knew this was already being done by the cops on the scene, but she wanted to hear the evidence, too.

It was getting scary. The killer had started out murdering the women a good six weeks apart. But the last two murders had had a time interval of only about ten days.

She wondered who would be next.

AS ALWAYS, Wynn had hoped for a quiet weekend on Fire Island and had instead been inundated by friends and business associates from Seventh Avenue. He managed to spend Saturday quietly—a walk on the beach, part of a book read while he lay in the hammock on the front porch of his house. But by Saturday evening people started to drop by for drinks until, by ten, his house resembled a party.

The usual garment industry people were there, plus numerous models—some escorted, some not. A musical comedy star had dropped in with her third husband of the decade. Most of the women were beautiful and all were well, if scantily, dressed.

For no reason at all he found himself thinking about the improbable blonde at Le Club—improbable because the color of her hair didn't suit her at all. Nobody, in his experience, had hair that color with eyes as dark as hers.

He couldn't help thinking what a sensation he would cause if he invited her out for the weekend. He could picture her wearing some totally unsuitable outfit and not even realizing it was unsuitable. The men would be amused at his choice, except for a few, perhaps, who would look further than her clothes and her hair and maybe see in her what he was seeing, an attitude he wasn't used to encountering, an attitude that stated that it was possible that everything he worked for had no importance in the scheme of things after all. The women would never understand, if they saw her at all. They were so used to just seeing clothes that they might miss her completely.

He didn't know what it was about her that kept her on his mind. He was sure that if he looked around him at work, or on the streets, he would see other women like her. He thought perhaps it was the incongruity of seeing this particular woman in the unlikely setting of Le Club.

It wasn't snobbery; it was a fact of life. Women went to Le Club to be seen, and this woman clearly didn't know that. Or, if she did, she didn't care, and that was intriguing, too.

He must be very bored with his life if one disastrously dressed woman could take hold of his mind while he was surrounded by some of the most beautiful women in the city.

But why did beautiful women always have to be so boring?

Chapter Three

It bothered Terry that none of the latest victim's neighbors claimed to have seen or heard anything. But that was Manhattan, and she should've been used to it by now. If the crime had happened in Brooklyn, it would've been a different story. At least one woman would have been leaning out of a window of the building, probably yelling at her kids. A couple of people would have been sitting on the stoop that hot summer evening and they would have observed everything that happened in the block.

Manhattan was a different story. Everyone minded his own business; no one wanted to get involved. Terry didn't think she would want to live in a place where people cared so little for each other. She might wish her neighbors weren't so nosy, but that very nosiness provided a sense of security, be it false or not.

Terry called Joy Freeman before she went to the precinct on Monday morning, hoping to catch the woman before she left for work.

"I'm calling about a friend of yours," Terry told her, after identifying herself as a police detective. "Janet Frame."

"Jan? Is she in trouble?"

Terry swallowed, hating the job of being the one to break the bad news. "I'm afraid she's been killed."

There was a shocked silence, then, "Killed? How?"

"I imagine you've read in the paper about the stranglings?"

"My God, Jan was strangled?"

"I'm really sorry to be the one to tell you. I wonder if it would be possible for us to have lunch together today. I'd like to ask you some questions about Ms. Frame."

It was arranged, and Terry spent the morning going over the interviews with the neighbors, none of which revealed anything except that Janet Frame evidently kept to herself.

Terry didn't have any problem recognizing Joy Freeman when she entered the coffee shop. She was as lovely and slim as the other members of Le Club.

When they had introduced themselves and ordered, Terry said, "What I'm going to tell you must be confidential, Ms. Freeman. We have reason to believe whoever's strangling these women is connected in some way to Le Club. I'm saying this because you might see me there, and since I'm working under cover, it would not be to my advantage if you recognized me."

"Don't worry," Joy assured her. "If the killings are connected to Le Club, I don't intend getting within fifty feet of that place again."

"Do you know what time Janet worked out on Friday night?" The medical examiner had placed the time of death as between eight and ten that night.

What the woman said next surprised her. "Jan didn't work out on Fridays. We both went Tuesdays, Thursdays and Saturdays, although we miss a lot of Saturdays in the summer. We did it mostly to avoid Mondays, which are really crowded."

That meant that the women weren't necessarily killed on their workout nights, which was something Terry would have to check. "Do you know if she was dating anyone from Le Club?"

"No, she was seeing someone from her office. Oh, God—Hugh probably doesn't even know about it yet."

"It was in the papers this morning."

"I can't believe he had to find out that way. Going to work and reading in the newspaper that Jan was killed." Tears sprang to her eyes and Terry gave her time to calm down.

"You don't think it possible she could've gone out with someone from Le Club?"

"What for? She was crazy about Hugh. Anyway, I've known her for years. She went steady in high school, steady in college, and now she's going with Hugh. She would never have cheated on any of them."

After lunch, which neither of them touched, Terry got together with Kyle and Lieutenant Corbet and told them what she had found out. "I think we're going to have to cover the club every night," she said, and they agreed with her. "The thing is," she added, "it might look strange. I was told the first night that you're supposed to skip a day, give the muscles a chance to rest."

"So they think we're gung ho," said Kyle. "It's better than letting the guy slip through our fingers."

That night Terry took her swimsuit along with her. As soon as she entered the exercise area, she went over to speak to Scott. "Is it really bad for you if you work out every night?" she asked him.

"Can't get enough of this place, huh?" Scott asked her with a grin.

He was so good-looking when he smiled that he almost took her breath away. "I enjoy it," she said, hoping that would satisfy as an explanation.

"Well, I'll tell you what, Terry. The thing to do is concentrate on your upper body and your lower body on alternate nights. And that way you'll have time to use the sauna and the pool."

Since the machines for her lower body were her favorites, she decided to concentrate on that area three nights and on the upper body the other two. Saturdays were out. She was definitely spending her weekends at home.

She tried to convince herself that the reason she had brought her swimsuit was that it was a real scorcher out that day and a swim would feel good, but she wasn't so self-deluding that she didn't know she was hoping to see Wynn Ransome at the pool.

But hell, it wasn't every day a man like that spoke to her. In fact, it never happened. The men she came in contact with were either criminals or cops or family members, none of whom drew her interest in the least. Wynn was like someone she'd seen in a movie and hoped to meet in person.

What would probably happen when she ran into him again would be that he'd ignore her, and after a while she'd begin to wonder if she'd imagined the whole thing.

Wynn almost didn't recognize her when she walked into the pool area, then realized it was because she had all that blond hair up under a swimming cap. For some reason, with the hair gone she looked all of a piece.

He noticed her surprised look as she glanced around, no doubt seeing that she was the only female present eschewing a bikini in favor of a tank suit so she could swim more easily. And, in fact, it was the first time he'd ever seen a swimming cap being worn at Le Club—but then, the other females never got their hair wet. Mostly they just hung around the pool, occasionally immersing themselves up to the neck, either to cool off or because they thought they looked sexier with wet fabric clinging to their bodies. Those same women might be serious when it came to the machines, but the pool was well known for being a purely social scene.

He caught her eye and nodded, but she quickly looked away. She dove into the pool, emerging at about the halfway mark, and did an ungainly stroke to reach the deep end of the pool. Somehow, with the suit and the cap, he had expected her to be a proficient swimmer, but if he wasn't mistaken, that was the dog paddle she was doing.

He watched her tread water for a moment; then he dove into the pool and broke the surface beside her. "How's it going?" he asked her, aware of the eyes now turning in their direction. Well, let them look. If they could figure out why he was attracted to her, it was more than he could do. All he knew was that she seemed to be the only one at the pool who was even half alive.

She looked at him, her eyes huge and dark in her small face. "Doesn't anyone swim?" she asked him, her eyes going to all the people surrounding the pool, and then to the pool itself, empty except for them.

"We seem to have it all to ourselves. Want to race to the end?"

"Sure, why not?" she said, and then started toward the shallow end.

He beat her easily, and when she pulled up he said, "That the only stroke you know?"

A light seemed to come on behind her eyes. "I don't think you could even call it a stroke."

"Shame on your swimming instructor. You've got the strength, but you're wasting your energy."

She smiled, the first time he had ever seen her smile. Her face magically turned from seriously calm to impudent, and she was almost laughing when she said, "No swimming instructor—just my father. His idea of teaching a kid to swim is to throw you in the water and whatever you do to save yourself, that's swimming."

He didn't know anyone who hadn't been given swimming lessons as a child, but she always seemed to be different. "Want a few pointers?" he asked.

"Sure. I'd like to learn that stroke you were doing."

Fifteen minutes later she still couldn't beat him, but her breaststroke looked like the result of more than one quick lesson. She was naturally coordinated, and she was really putting some effort into it.

She pulled herself up to sit by the side of the pool and he joined her. He saw some people almost imperceptibly pull closer, as though to hear what he had to talk about with this woman.

"My name's Wynn, by the way," he told her.

She nodded her head. "I know. Someone told me the first night I was here. Then my sister told me who you were."

"Well, since no one told me your name..."

"Terry. Terry Caputo."

"You asked your sister about me?" he asked, curious.

"The person who told me your name made it sound as though I should know who you were. That remark I made about clothes being a waste of money—that must have sounded pretty rude to you."

"I'm sure it was the truth."

"Yes. But I could've just kept my mouth shut."

He had a feeling that wasn't something she was in the habit of doing. He was also picking up on something else, surprised that he hadn't noticed it before. She had a New York accent, not a strong one, but it was there nonetheless. He was so used to New York accents on Seventh Avenue that it hadn't hit him before. But at Le Club? He figured she was probably the only one there who wasn't originally from someplace else.

"What are you doing later?" he asked her, not even attempting to understand his reason for asking.

He expected her to say she had plans, but all she said was "Going home." She didn't even try to make him think she had a busy social life.

"Want to get something to eat?"

He could see by the expressions crossing her face that she was trying to find a way out of it, but finally, after what seemed like a long silence, she said, "Okay."

Not "I'd love to"; she was not feigning interest in any way. Instead, she sounded more as if she was giving in only because she couldn't think of any excuse not to.

"Good. Unless you want to swim some more, I'll meet you in front in about twenty minutes. That enough time for you?"

She just nodded, so he got up and headed for the locker room. He'd take her to Elaine's. He felt comfortable there and Elaine would give him preferential treatment, one of the good tables. Plus, he was looking forward to the reactions of some of his friends when he walked into Elaine's with an unknown, especially the kind of unknown they weren't accustomed to.

He had a feeling, and he could be wrong about this, of course—but he had a feeling that she didn't have the kind of money the others at Le Club had. It wasn't her clothes. He could be thrown off by clothes; some of the richest people he knew dressed worse than she did. And it wasn't her attitude, because she was as self-possessed as anyone he knew. He knew it was partly the accent, which was pretty snobbish of him, but the fact of the matter was, New Yorkers with money usually got rid of their accents somewhere along the way, generally in private schools.

But if she didn't have money, what the hell was she doing at Le Club? Granted, she seemed serious about working out, but there were lots of health clubs in the city and almost all of them cost a lot less.

Anyway, Elaine's ought to be a treat for her. Not that it wouldn't be a treat for him, too—partly to see her reactions, but also because it had been a while since he had been out with a woman who wasn't totally predictable.

It might be an interesting evening.

TERRY SPENT MOST of the twenty minutes trying to find Kyle to alert him that she was leaving with one of the members. She finally located him in the sauna, surrounded by beautiful females, and he didn't look thrilled to see her. Still, when she gave the signal they had worked out he gave the answering one, and when she emerged from the building she saw him already across the street, trying to blend into the scenery.

Kyle was one of the reasons she hadn't wanted to accept the invitation. She knew she was going to hear the next day at work about the fact that she was using the job to date someone, even though it was only dinner. Kyle would think it a waste of his time, which it no doubt was.

She didn't care, though; she'd risk the hard time she was in for from Kyle. It was such a rarity to be asked out by a man who was both intelligent and a gentleman that she would have hated to turn Wynn down. That she was attracted to him was a bonus.

She dressed in her jeans and cotton shirt, putting her hair in a long braid since it had gotten wet despite the bathing cap. Still, her hair hadn't turned green. Kathy had warned her that sometimes bleached hair turned green from the chlorine in pools, and Kathy ought to know since she had been experimenting with bleaching her own hair since her teenage years. Terry's clothes had been another reason she had wanted to say no, but when Wynn came out of the building he was also in jeans and a cotton shirt, so she relaxed about that.

Mostly, though, she hadn't felt ready to see Wynn alone, outside the confines of Le Club. She had thought about seeing him, but that thought had been in the realm of fantasy, not something she thought would actually take place. He seemed too well known to be asking her out; she had never been out with a celebrity before, and according to Kathy, Wynn was famous.

His status might have made her suspicious of him, or of his reasons for choosing her to go out with, except that Terry still couldn't see him as the strangler. Why would someone teach her how to swim and then try to kill her? It didn't make sense. But then, strangling women didn't make sense anyway.

He asked her if she preferred to walk or take a cab, and she opted to walk, partly because she felt like walking and partly so that Kyle would have an easier time of following them—and maybe a little bit because she knew Kyle would hate having to walk.

They headed uptown on Second Avenue and she kept expecting Wynn to stop at one of the restaurants. But they kept walking, neither of them saying anything, until finally he asked her what she did for a living.

She'd be damned if she was going to say that she did nothing, hating the image of a rich woman who did nothing with her life, so she said, "Interior decorating," trying to sound offhand about it.

He looked over at her. "I wouldn't have figured you for that."

That made him more astute than the lieutenant, Terry thought. "What would you have figured me for?"

"I don't know; just not that. It's hard to believe that someone who thinks clothes are a waste of money doesn't feel the same about furniture and curtains and matching wallpaper."

He was right; she thought decorating was a waste of money, too. And he sure wasn't going to forget that remark of hers. Not wanting to get into a discussion of respective jobs, she tried to think of something else to talk about, but nothing came to mind. It was tricky being with a man she didn't know when she couldn't discuss her police work, didn't want to have to discuss interior decorating and wasn't particularly interested in what he did. She finally decided that Le Club was a safe topic and asked him what he thought of the place.

"A bit pretentious, but a good facility," he said.

She thought it was more than a bit pretentious, but didn't voice her opinion. "How long you been going there?"

"A few years. Before it became the 'in' place to go. I went to school with one of the owners and he got me interested in Nautilus machines before they became so popular."

She wondered if he meant high school or college, and decided he meant college, which was another subject she wouldn't bring up. "I like the machines. They're a lot more fun than free weights."

"You've worked out with free weights?" he asked.

Since that would only lead to the subject of the Brooklyn YMCA, Terry just nodded and decided it was safer to walk in silence.

He finally chose a restaurant, but it looked so ordinary she wondered why they had walked so far to get there. A heavyset woman greeted him by name, then led them to one of the tables. About half the tables were filled, and some of the people nodded to Wynn or said hello. When they were seated and handed menus, Terry saw that Kyle had come in and taken a seat at the bar.

The place didn't look Italian but it had an Italian menu, and Wynn said the spaghetti was good, so she ordered that and agreed to share a bottle of wine with him.

When the food came and she found out how bad it was, she decided he must live in the neighborhood and came there out of convenience. At least she couldn't think of any other reason why he might eat there.

Once she looked up from her plate and saw that some of the people at other tables were looking at her. She thought it was paranoia, then decided it really wasn't, because some of them were actually staring.

She glanced over at Wynn, and when he asked her what was the matter she said, "Why are people staring at us? Are you that famous?"

"They're wondering who you are," he said, ignoring the reference to his fame.

"But why?"

"They're trying to place you, that's all."

She looked over at the bar to see if people were trying to place Kyle, but no one seemed to be paying any attention to him. She decided that if this was what going out with a celebrity entailed, she'd forget it.

She might be physically attracted to Wynn, but mentally they didn't seem to have a thing in common, and eating in near silence wasn't her idea of a good time. It would have been easier, of course, if she could just tell him who she was and maybe talk about her work. But since she couldn't, the whole thing was beginning to seem like a waste of time.

Once they were out of Elaine's, though, and walking home, it got better. He took hold of her hand as though it were the most natural thing in the world to do, and for some reason the conversation became easier. Maybe it had just been Elaine's, being stared at. He started making joking remarks about things in the store windows and pretty soon she was doing the same thing. They were both laughing by the time they turned onto her street.

She found herself getting a little nervous as they approached her door. She wondered if he expected to be asked in, wondered if she wanted to ask him in. But in the end he had just squeezed her hand and told her he had enjoyed himself.

Later, when Terry described the evening to Kathy, it sounded more interesting than it had actually been.

"You were at Elaine's?" asked Kathy, sounding excited about it for some reason.

"Yeah, you heard of the place?"

"Everyone's heard of Elaine's."

"Well, I don't know why," said Terry. "The food was sure lousy."

"You don't go there for the food. You go to be seen."

"I was seen all right. In fact I was stared at."

"That's because you were with Wynn Ransome. They probably thought you were someone famous they should recognize."

"How do you know all this stuff, Kath? You never even get out of Brooklyn."

"I read *People* magazine. You ought to read it, Terry."

"What for? I don't think I'll be seeing him again."

"You blew it, right?"

"There was nothing to blow. I don't know, Kath—maybe it's because I'm not used to going out with a man, but I thought it was a disaster. I couldn't talk about my work or my family or my background. It was just no good; we had nothing to talk about."

"You should've asked him about his work."

"I'm not interested in his work."

"Well, you've got to pretend an interest."

"Why do I have to do that?"

"You're impossible, Terry. You always were," referring, no doubt, to all the advice she had given her when Terry had been in high school. Terry had ignored it all.

"What I don't see is why a guy would go into designing women's clothes. I thought designers were all gay."

"Most of them are."

"But, then why would Wynn be interested in designing?"

"His father owned the business and Wynn took over when he died."

There was a pause, then, "I think you ought to be the one going out with him. Are you telling me you learned that in *People*?"

"He's been written up a lot, Terry."

It was beginning to annoy her that her sister knew more about Wynn than she did, so she said, "How's it going with Johnny?"

"I can't talk about it right now," she said, her voice the merest whisper.

Her response meant Johnny was home, so Terry promised to call her sister the next day, then got off the phone.

When she got to work the next day, Kyle was complaining to Lieutenant Corbet about having to follow Terry around while she dated guys from Le Club.

Terry walked in on them and said, "Not guys, Kyle—I've only gone out once."

"You think it's anything, Terry?" the lieutenant asked her.

"If you mean do I think he's the strangler, no. He didn't even ask to come in, just left me at my door."

"He's the only one she even talks to there," Kyle said, complaining further.

"That right, Terry?" the lieutenant asked.

"He's the only one who talks to me. What do you want me to do, start flirting with all the guys?"

"If necessary, yes," she was told, and she saw Kyle smirking at her.

"I'm not very good at that," Terry said.

"Terry," Lieutenant Corbet said, "if you were on decoy as a hooker, I'd expect you to approach the men. In the same way, you should be treating Le Club for what it is—a place to meet men. But you've got to meet them halfway."

Terry began to balk at that, then backed down. "If they were interested, they'd flirt with me."

"This is the eighties, Terry. Women are allowed to make the first move."

"All right. I'll be a little more friendly."

"Be a *lot* more friendly," Lieutenant Corbet ordered.

Terry fumed, but she didn't argue. There was only so much arguing the lieutenant would tolerate before he came down hard on you.

But she wasn't pleased. A perfectly nice man was showing an interest in her and now, in front of him, she was expected to start flirting with every other man in the place. She was going to feel very stupid and probably end up antagonizing Wynn.

Not that there was any possibility of it going anywhere with Wynn. She was kidding herself if she thought that being honest with him would make it any better. A fashion designer and a cop wasn't a likely combination.

That night she started smiling at the men in the club, but the only one who even spoke to her was Scott, and that was to tell her she was using one of the machines wrong.

On Wednesday, what they hoped wouldn't happen, did. One of the morning newspapers broke the story that the strangler was picking on women from Le Club. That night, when she got to the locker room, the women were talking of nothing else. She overheard one blonde say, "I don't know about you guys, but I think I might change clubs."

When she got to the exercycles she saw Lisa and took the one next to her.

"I guess you heard the news," Lisa said, sounding more serious than usual.

Terry nodded.

"You going to keep on coming here?"

"I don't know. What about you?"

"I'll tell you one thing, I'm in no mood to exercise tonight. Want to go to Bloomingdale's? They're having a sale on swimwear. I could use a new suit."

That sounded good to Terry. She had never seen Bloomingdale's and was curious about it, and leaving with Lisa would also mean she wouldn't have to flirt with the men that night—or run into Wynn.

But then she remembered what the lieutenant had said, and she asked Lisa, "How about if we work out for a half hour before we leave?" When Lisa agreed, Terry's conscience was assuaged somewhat.

So for a half hour she smiled at every man who crossed her path and, except for a couple of halfhearted smiles in return, she didn't get anywhere with her flirting.

When she signalled Kyle that she was leaving alone, she saw his look of surprise that she didn't intend to work out longer. But he looked pretty happy where he was—coincidentally, of course, in the company of three women.

Bloomingdale's was a revelation, living up to all its advertising. There was even a department devoted to WIN clothing, which Lisa pointed out to her on the way to the swimwear department.

Terry thought the bathing suits, even at half price, were outrageously expensive. But she bought one anyway, a tank with wide stripes of blue and yellow and white. Lisa told her it was a Ralph Lauren, which didn't mean anything to Terry, but at least it wasn't one of Wynn's. She'd have felt really stupid showing up at the pool in one of his.

They got something to eat at the coffee shop in the store, then Lisa asked her if she wanted to go to a movie that was playing across the street. Terry thought it sounded better than going home and watching TV, so she agreed.

Terry really enjoyed the movie. It had been a long time since she had seen anything but children's movies, or Mike's favorite science fiction. It was also nice being out with a friend. She hadn't had a female friend since her school days and she found it was something she had missed.

"I hear you left with Wynn the other night," Lisa said when they were having coffee after the movie.

"How'd you hear that?" Terry wanted to know.

"You were seen, that's how. What'd you think, you were invisible? Half the women there have their eyes on him."

"We went out to eat," said Terry.

"Where'd you go?"

"Elaine's."

"I'm impressed."

"Don't be, the food was lousy."

Lisa laughed. "Come on, Terry, no one goes there for the food. So what happened? I thought you weren't interested."

"He seems pretty nice."

Lisa's eyes widened. "He seems pretty nice? You go out with Wynn Ransome and all you can say is that he seems pretty nice?"

"It wasn't all that great, Lisa. I couldn't even think of anything to talk about."

"Any other woman would have been out to charm him to death."

"I'm not the charming type."

"Well, make an effort."

"Look, Lisa, can I level with you?"

"Sure."

"I'm serious. I'm going to tell you something that has to stay between us."

Lisa's eyes lit up as though she were going to be told a juicy tidbit about Wynn. "I can keep a secret, Terry."

"I'm a cop."

"You're a *what*?" Lisa said, doing a double take at this totally unexpected revelation.

"A detective. Homicide. I'm at Le Club under cover because of the stranglings."

Lisa just stared at her for a few moments before saying, "That's the most exciting thing I've ever heard."

"This isn't a movie, Lisa. It's real. And if you want my advice, I'd quit going there until we catch the guy."

"You really are a cop?"

Terry nodded. "Which makes the whole thing with Wynn so ridiculous. Could you see him being interested in a cop?"

Lisa looked as if she wanted to say yes, but finally shook her head. "It doesn't seem likely."

Terry, relieved to get it out in the open, said, "I've got to act like some rich playgirl who does interior decorating, and I don't know the first thing about either. And so when I'm with him I hardly say anything, because anything I say is a lie."

"I can see where that would be a problem. I think being a cop's a lot more interesting than being an interior decorator, though."

"People at Elaine's were staring at me, trying to figure out what he saw in me. Hell, I was trying to figure it out, too."

"The whole club's trying to figure it out. Hey, I didn't mean that like it sounded. It's just that he usually ignores the women there, and he's always gone for model types in his personal life."

"How do you know that?"

"Everyone knows it. But that's probably because he works with a lot of models. Just like you probably go out with cops."

"I was married to one," Terry said. "That's another thing. I'm a widow with a twelve-year-old son, which I'm sure would be another shock to him."

"It's a shock to me," said Lisa. "You don't look old enough to have a son that age."

"I got married practically right out of high school."

"You really are a dark horse, aren't you? Well, listen, Terry. Look at it this way: If Wynn's the type who doesn't like cops and kids, then you don't want him anyway."

Terry sighed. "I guess."

"But enjoy it while it lasts."

"That's another thing. I'm now supposed to start flirting with all the guys there to try to smoke out the strangler."

"Which is going to be a real insult to Wynn."

"Yeah, and he doesn't deserve it."

"It's going to make things interesting at Le Club."

"I really think you should stop going there, Lisa."

"Don't worry, I'll be careful. I don't think anyone is going to do much dating there for the duration. Particularly those of us with blond hair."

Terry started to smile. "I have one final confession to make."

"Another?"

"I'm not even a blonde."

"You didn't have to tell me that. I've seen you in the shower, remember? But so what? Half the blondes there aren't natural."

"Yeah, but Wynn also thinks I'm a blonde."

"I wouldn't be so sure of that. Anyway, I bet you look terrific with dark hair."

"I really appreciate your listening to me, Lisa. I needed someone to talk to."

"Hell, what're friends for?"

Terry wasn't sure what friends were for. She had family, and she relied on them, although sometimes they managed to annoy her unreasonably. She had the men she worked with, but she couldn't really say they were friends. The men on the squad made friends with each other, but she was the only female and they treated her differently. They were either extremely businesslike with her—sometimes unsuccessfully hiding a trace of resentment that she was even with homicide—or they treated her the way they treated all women, as an object of sexual interest only.

She was glad she had met Lisa. They exchanged phone numbers, and Terry felt that it would be nice to have someone outside her family to talk to, someone who wouldn't dump family problems in her lap.

WHEN TERRY GOT TO Le Club the following night she saw that the ranks of blond members had been noticeably depleted. She was sure it was a result of a follow-up article in one of the newspapers—a scare piece that Terry was afraid might cause panic at the club. In fact, it looked as though some of the non-blondes had also stayed away.

That, she reasoned, might make it easier for her. The fewer targets the strangler had to choose from, the better were her chances of being chosen.

Scott stopped her on the way to the cycles and said, "You know, Terry, you might try running on alternate nights. Those cycles get pretty monotonous. Why don't you give it a try? Just a mile or two to start off with."

Thinking anything would be more interesting than the exercycles, Terry went up the steps to the track and joined the small group of men who were running in circles. Some of them wore Walkmans on their heads, others ran to the piped-in music.

After a half mile she knew she was enjoying it more than the exercycles, but she also realized that her sneakers weren't the right shoes for running. She would go shopping on Saturday for running shoes, maybe buy Mike a new pair at the same time.

None of the men seemed to be paying any attention to her as they passed her on the track, and she tried to give some thought to how she was supposed to flirt with them when they were all involved in what they were doing to the exclusion of everything else.

Later, when she was using the free weights, a man did speak to her. He gave her some pointers and even offered to spot her, and when they were finished and she was wondering if he was going to suggest getting together, he surprised her by telling her that his girlfriend was a serious bodybuilder. So much for flirting, she thought, although she hadn't really flirted with the man; she had just been friendly.

She knew there was a restaurant in the building housing Le Club and decided to get something to eat there before going home, thinking that maybe the killer met his quarries there. But except for having to eat food that was only slightly better than Elaine's, nothing of interest happened.

On Friday, Terry decided that maybe the killer went for the ballerina look and, despite feeling foolish, she did some quick shopping. She showed up in the exercise room that night in black leotard and tights. All she got out of it, though, was a look of approval from the woman in the locker room and a look of amazement from Lisa.

"You decided to conform, I see," said Lisa as they made the circuit together.

Terry looked around for Wynn and was thankful that she didn't see him. "It's all in the interests of my job," she said.

"You really think the strangler cares how you dress? He's got to be some kind of a nut."

"Maybe he goes for blond ballerinas. Who knows? I'm not getting anywhere with flirting because either I'm not doing it right or they're just not interested."

"They're interested, all right. You've just got to be subtle. Pick out a guy you're interested in and then ignore him."

"I've been ignoring all of them."

"I said you had to be subtle, Terry. The guy's got to be aware you're ignoring him. It has to make him wonder if maybe there's something wrong with him."

"Are you serious, Lisa?"

"Sure. You've got to use psychology on them. Like your remark to Wynn. It might not have been meant as a come-on, but you've got to admit it worked."

It didn't make any sense to Terry. How could she subtly ignore men who were totally ignoring her in the first place?

She finished up early that night and was heading out of the building when she met Wynn coming in. He was in a shirt and tie, his suit jacket over his arm, and he looked different to her in business clothes. More serious. Just as handsome, but a little intimidating.

"You finished already?" he asked her, pausing in front of the steps.

She wished now she had stayed longer, even looking like a dumb ballerina. Hell, maybe he liked the look. "I got an early start," she lied, not wanting to explain that she now came to the club every night so she finished earlier.

He set down the canvas bag he was carrying and looked in no hurry to leave. "What're you doing this weekend?"

As soon as he said it her eagerness to get home dissipated and, for the first time since Mike was born, she found herself wishing she was free of responsibilities. "I spend weekends on my boat," she told him. Then she smiled to herself, thinking she should have used the word "yacht," but also knowing she would have laughed out loud if she had. Her boat bore absolutely no resemblance to a yacht.

His first look of surprise changed to one of interest. "Where do you keep it?"

"Mill Basin Marina."

"I don't think I've heard of that."

"It's in Brooklyn," she told him, seeing by his face that she might as well have said Outer Mongolia.

He reached down to pick up his bag and said, "Well, maybe we could get together Monday night."

She was surprised that he was pursuing what she thought was a dead-end relationship. But since he was, she suddenly wanted to press the advantage. "Why don't you come over to my place for dinner Monday?" she asked, belatedly wondering how Lieutenant Corbet would react to her invitation.

Wynn was reacting quite well. Smiling, he said, "That'd be great."

"Good," she said, grinning back at him.

"Well, enjoy your weekend."

"Thanks. You too." Maybe she would, with this to look forward to.

She waited for him to go into the building before getting into her Jeep, which was parked out in front. She hated to admit it to herself, but her former eagerness to get home and see Mike had been somewhat lessened by the knowledge that she had the whole weekend to get through before she'd see Wynn again.

Her assessment made it sound as if she was getting more involved than she would like. But still, she couldn't keep a big smile from spreading across her face, even when the damn Jeep wouldn't start on the first try.

Watch out, you're falling for the guy, she told herself as she finally drove off.

Still, if anything came of it, it would be the first work-related benefit she had ever got.

Chapter Four

A boat in Brooklyn? She continued to be full of surprises, thought Wynn. For some reason he hadn't thought she was the boating type, but maybe he too freely categorized people. And yet, until he'd met Terry Caputo, he thought he'd been able to read people fairly well.

And it pretty much smashed his theory that she couldn't afford Le Club.

The only thing he knew about Brooklyn was that a long time ago it had had its own baseball team. Yes, and there was a place there called Coney Island, although he wasn't sure it was still around. But a marina? He thought those were all on Long Island.

So, what did he have here? A woman who could afford to be a member of Le Club; one whose clothes looked more like Lerner's than Bergdorf's; who was plain-speaking if she spoke at all, and she didn't seem to be much on trivial conversation; and now he had found out that she spent weekends in Brooklyn on a boat. That would no doubt account for the New York accent.

Her name, now—Caputo. That would be Italian, he supposed. And an Italian with money could possibly mean Mafia. Or perhaps he had seen too many movies. Certainly everyone bearing Italian surnames were not Mafia-connected, were they? And yet that would explain the money, and the certain air of mystery about her, because there definitely was that.

The invitation to dinner on Monday has been a surprise. It had been equally surprising that he had been so pleased by the invitation. It had been amusing to take her to Elaine's and cause a little talk, but there would be no one to see them at her place. Yet he was still looking forward to it.

He'd better watch himself or he'd become more involved than he intended becoming. Granted, he was pretty tired of models and even more tired of their conversations but that didn't mean he had to fall for the first nonmodel he came in contact with. The city was full of single women, and most of them weren't models. In fact most of the female members of Le Club weren't models, although they tried their best to look as if they were.

And yet, when he was sketching some new designs that afternoon, he had found himself sketching Terry wearing the clothes. Not Terry with all that blond hair, but Terry with her hair pulled back into a long braid the way she'd been wearing it on Wednesday night. At the exact time he realized what he was doing, whom he was drawing, he also realized something else. His clothes looked better on her than on the conventional models he used. He didn't know why that was so, but it was.

He had called in his assistant, Meg, and asked her what she thought.

"I like them," she said, admiring the designs.

"No, I'm talking about the model. What do you think?"

Meg took a closer look. "She doesn't look like a model."

"Exactly. But what's your reaction?"

"I'd say the clothes suit her. Probably more than they suit the high-fashion models we use. There's a tomboyish appeal about her, almost an urchin look, that's just right with that outfit. The other models tend to make the clothes look high-fashion, which they really aren't."

"I was thinking the same thing," said Wynn. "Let's find some models who look more like this."

Meg was shaking her head. "But models don't look like that. Girls who look like that don't go into modeling."

"Then find some nonmodels who look like that and get them to model. I'll also want to talk to our advertising agency. I have an idea for a whole new concept."

"Are you sure about this?" Meg asked.

"Very sure. As for the models—no blondes."

Meg took another look at his drawing. "But she's a blonde."

"Maybe, but she shouldn't be." He quickly filled in the hair in the sketch, making it black, then nodded in satisfaction. "That's what I want—exactly like that."

Meg just went away shaking her head.

When Terry got home Pop was out again, and Mike, clearly bored, was complaining he hadn't been fed.

"We'll go for pizza," said Terry, not in the mood to cook.

"And a movie. Could we go to a movie afterward, Mom?"

"Why not?" she said, thinking it sounded better than staying home and wondering what Wynn was doing.

It wasn't better. It was another science fiction movie, and Terry didn't think she was going to be satisfied with Mike's choices of movies much longer, especially after having so enjoyed the movie she had seen on Wednesday night with Lisa. To add insult to injury, Mike told her afterward that it was the third time he'd seen this particular film. But Mike would rather see something he was sure he liked than take a chance on an unknown.

All through the movie she had been thinking of telling him about Wynn, but she reconsidered because of an incident that occurred when they were in an ice-cream shop after the show. Two guys walked by their booth and made some smart remark about "blond bimbos," which Mike, of course, immediately picked up on.

"Why were they looking at you, Mom?" he wanted to know.

"'Cause they're stupid."

"Yeah, but they were looking at you like you were a girl."

"Well, I'm not a boy, Mike."

"Yeah, but you're a mother."

She saw that he really was angry. "Mike, just because I'm a mother doesn't make me an old lady yet. A lot of women my age go out on dates, you know."

He gave her his you've-got-to-be-kidding look. "You don't do that," he said.

Terry sighed. Now was clearly not the time to bring up Wynn. Or even men in general. Still, Mike needed a little straightening out. "Your grandfather dates. And I might start dating one of these days. You never know."

"Dating's stupid," was all Mike had to say about that.

THE NEXT DAY Mike was out with his friends and Terry was cleaning the boat when Pop stopped by.

"How's the case coming, Terry?" he asked.

"It isn't, Pop, but I'm sure developing muscles," she said, flexing one arm for him to see.

"Muscles don't become a woman," he said. That was the kind of remark she didn't like to hear from him. Her expression must have shown it because he added, "So I'm old-fashioned. Sue me."

"Everyone's working out these days, Pop."

Her father, who had been a longshoreman, said, "Work used to be enough."

"Maybe your kind of work."

Pop was looking nervous, which wasn't like him. She offered him a beer, and he went and got it himself. Then, after he took a long swallow, he said, "There's someone I want you to meet."

At last she was going to hear about the girlfriend. "Who's that, Pop?"

"Someone I'm seeing," he said, almost mumbling the words.

"The mystery lady, huh?" she teased, then wished she hadn't because his face seemed to close up.

"She's never seen where I live," he said, which explained it. Obviously the woman was curious, maybe even thought she was dating a married man, and since Pop was forced into showing her his boat, and since he knew he couldn't do that without all the neighbors seeing, he had decided to come out in the open.

"What's her name, Pop?"

"Cindi."

That seemed like an awfully cute name for a friend of Pop's. "So when do I get to meet her?"

He was looking everywhere but at Terry. "I thought maybe Sunday afternoon."

"Mike and I are going to the aunts' for dinner." Terry had arranged the date the week after she found out from Kathy that aunts Rosa and Anna were feeling neglected.

Pop, acting embarrassed, cleared his throat and said, "Well, you could stop by after breakfast, I guess."

That had to mean the woman was going to be spending the night on his boat. It wouldn't be the first time it had occurred, but for some reason he was making a production out of it this time, which might mean it was serious.

"How long you been seeing her, Pop?"

"You mean Cindi?"

"Of course I mean Cindi. That's who we're talking about, isn't it?"

"For a while."

Well, if he wanted to be secretive, let him. She'd reserve judgment until she met the woman on Sunday. Although by the way he was carrying on she had to figure this one was more important to him than the others had been.

That night, with Mike staying over at a friend's house and Pop perhaps already home with Cindi, Terry began to feel a dissatisfaction with her life. That was unusual. She was happy with her work, she certainly loved her son, and living on the boat had grown on her until she no longer even thought about finding an apartment.

She realized that for the first time in years she was feeling a need for something more. The problem was, she had been given a taste of another way of life, and she found she liked it. Not that she'd really want to be an interior decorator, or even a rich playgirl. She enjoyed police work and had no quarrel with that. Plus, she thought her work had a value to it that she found lacking in things such as the decor of one's home, or even the style of one's clothes.

But she was enjoying her undercover work in the city, and that wasn't supposed to be for her enjoyment. Even the sublet, which at first she hadn't been crazy about, had its advantages. She was beginning to like the quiet, something she got little of with Mike around. She had taken to sitting out in the yard before going to bed at night. It was very quiet there, with only the faint sounds of traffic in the distance. It would be nice to have a garden like that—a place to invite friends over, maybe have a party. Or a place to entertain a lover? she found herself wondering. Was that really the reason for her sudden dissatisfaction?

All right, so she'd been living like a nun since Nick died. It wasn't out of choice, was it? She had met other men, both through family and through work, and it had been a toss-up which had been worse.

Kathy had paraded a string of Johnny's friends in front of her over the years, and they had all been cut from the same cloth. They were looking for someone to cook for them and take care of their houses, much as their mothers did, someone who would also take care of their needs when they weren't out with the boys at a ball game or just out drinking beer.

As for the other cops she had met, forget it. The best of them were marital risks, judging by the statistics that said cops got divorced more often than any other group of men. She didn't need that statistic, though, to tell her what she saw every day with her own eyes. There wasn't a married one of them who wasn't running around and thinking it his due. And they regarded women as they regarded their guns— they were something to use.

In fact, if she hadn't met Nick as a child, they probably wouldn't have ended up together. If she hadn't known him before he was a cop, she didn't think she would have fallen in love with him. It was something she didn't often think about, but during that last year before he was killed she had been pretty sure he was fooling around. She would have confronted him with it eventually, but his premature death had ended all speculation.

Wynn wasn't like any of the men she knew. For one thing, he was soft-spoken. He didn't make ordinary conversation sound like shouted orders and he appeared to be just as interested in what she had to say as he was in his own remarks. Not that she had had much to say, but that had been her fault, not his.

She liked his looks, too. There was no getting around the fact that Italian men were sexy; her own father was a good example of that. But along with those looks you had to take their macho attitude, and she had had enough macho men in her life. And it wasn't just the Italians, she had to admit; most Brooklyn men had that same aggressive attitude.

Wynn was like someone in a movie, or on TV. There was a fictional quality to him she couldn't quite define. He was also a gentleman, and that wasn't something she was used to. Not in any of his movements, not in anything he said, did he appear to be coming on to her. And yet he must be interested or why was he bothering?

Any other men she knew would have taken some advantage of her while they were in the swimming pool. At the least they would have made some suggestive remark. But that behavior was absent in Wynn, and as a result, she felt comfortable with him—excited by him in a way, but still comfortable. She knew she wasn't going to have to fight him off at some point.

It wasn't as though there was anything asexual about him. Far from it. The way his body moved, the gleam she sometimes caught in his eyes and those sexy eyes themselves, with their slightly downward slant, were all very sensual. And his smile, which seemed so warm and approving, also seemed to be tempting her in some way.

And if she didn't watch it, she was going to start acting like some high school girl with her first crush.

She was a grown woman with a son, a homicide detective—hell, just your average New Yorker. She ought to know better than to think she had a chance with some celebrity designer who must have half the women in the city after him.

It didn't hurt to dream, though. Pop had a new girlfriend. Even Mike appeared to be finally noticing the opposite sex. She wasn't dead yet, was she?

TERRY AWAKENED the next morning to the sound of Huey Lewis and the News and yelled to Mike to turn his radio down. When the noise didn't diminish, she rolled out of bed with a groan and made her way to the deck. There was no sign of Mike and she saw that the rowboat was gone.

Then she realized the music was coming from Pop's boat. Pop listening to Huey Lewis? It didn't make sense.

She dressed quickly, then went back out on the deck and was jumping over to Pop's boat when she remembered about Cindi. Well, if they were playing music they must be up, she figured, knocking on the cabin door before entering.

A young woman, dressed in what looked like one of Pop's V-necked T-shirts and a pair of bikini panties, was standing in the galley with a frying pan in her hand.

"You must be Terry," she said in a sweet little voice, and Terry was too startled to do anything but stare. If this was Cindi, she didn't look much older than Mike.

"Hi, I'm Cindi. Your dad said you'd be over. He went to the bakery, should be back in a sec."

Terry was still taking in the pleasingly plump contours, the layered hair that mostly obscured the round face, and the bright-green polished toenails on the bare feet, when she was asked if she'd like some coffee.

"Please," Terry managed to say. She sat down in one of the captain's chairs.

"Your dad's a real sweetie. All I had to do was mention the word 'Danish,' and he was off like a shot to buy some. You want some eggs? I'm fixing them scrambled."

"No thanks," said Terry. "Just coffee."

The girl poured a mug of coffee and carried it over to Terry. "I hear you're a police officer. I bet that must be exciting. I know Frankie's real proud of you."

For a moment Terry didn't know who Cindi was talking about, and then it dawned on her. But "Frankie"? No one had ever called Pop Frankie.

Not caring if she was being rude, Terry reached over and turned down the radio. "What do you do, Cindi?" she inquired, sounding even to herself like a nosy parent.

"I work the counter at Harry's Diner. That's where I met your dad. He comes in there for lunch a lot."

Terry was just digesting that bit of news when Pop got back, wearing a yachting cap that Terry had never seen him in before.

"So, my two girls have met, huh?" he asked. It was about the most inane remark Terry had ever heard him utter.

"We were just getting acquainted," said Cindi.

Terry felt as if she were in the middle of a TV sitcom. The aging parent, the young girlfriend, the disapproving daughter...

The only problem was, this was real.

Pop was putting the Danish on a plate when he seemed to notice that Cindi wasn't quite dressed. He said, "Why don't you put some clothes on, honey?" giving her a whack on the rear end, which made Cindi squeal and Terry cringe.

As soon as the girl disappeared into the bedroom, Terry said, "Is she of age, Pop?" She hadn't meant to sound sarcastic, but she knew it came out sounding that way.

"She's twenty-two, Terry, which makes her an adult."

"Has she shown you ID or are you taking her word for it?"

"Either show some respect, young lady, or mind your own business."

"You're the one who wanted me to meet her."

She could tell that Pop was dying to make some other remark, or maybe order her off the boat, but just then Cindi returned in shorts and a halter, which didn't cover her as much as what she had previously been wearing.

"Don't you just love this boat?" she asked Terry. "I think it's so romantic to be living on a boat."

Terry thought of water shortages and blown fuses and freezing cold toilet seats in the winter, and didn't answer her.

Pop said, "You joining us for breakfast, Terry?" and she could tell by the way he said it that he was hoping her answer would be no.

"Why not?" said Terry, getting a smile from Cindi and a scowl from Pop.

The conversation, though—mostly Cindi's—was enough to make her lose any appetite she might have had. If the girl had a brain in her head it wasn't discernible, yet Pop seemed to think she was the most entertaining thing to come his way since the demise of *The Ed Sullivan Show*.

Back on her boat, she couldn't wait to tell Kathy. As soon as she called her, Kathy started in on Johnny, but Terry interrupted her to say, "Wait'll you get a load of Pop's new girlfriend."

"You've met her?"

"In person. It seems she spent the night with him. Prepare yourself, Kath—she looks sixteen tops."

"Pop's dating a teenager?"

"He says she's twenty-two, but she sure doesn't look it. And to hear her talk, you'd think she was Mike's age. Maybe younger."

"He must be going through male menopause," said Kathy. "I've heard about it, but I didn't think it would happen to my own father."

"She's a waitress," Terry said.

"There's nothing wrong with that," said Kathy, who had once been a waitress during a summer vacation.

"I wasn't criticizing, just stating a fact. The thing is, Kathy, I think Pop's serious. You should see him—he's like a kid looking at his first ice-cream cone."

"I don't think I like that picture," said Kathy.

"Listen, I'm going to the aunts' for dinner, but why don't you and Johnny stop by and see Pop? Meet her for yourself. I'd love to hear your opinion of her."

"I think we'll do just that," Kathy said, and then she hung up to pass the news on to Johnny.

UNLIKE AUNT ANNA, whose existence, ever since her husband committed suicide by jumping off the Brooklyn Bridge, seemed doomed to be anticlimactic, Aunt Rosa was smiling and cheerful, and she'd always shown a preference for Terry.

"Come in," she said to them, giving Terry a big hug, then leading them into the crowded apartment the two aunts shared in the Flatbush section of Brooklyn.

Mike, who had successfully evaded his turn at a hug, was already in the living room in front of the TV when Terry got there after stopping to say hello to Aunt Anna in the kitchen.

Terry felt so at home here that she usually barely noticed the room. But this time she noted the clear plastic covers over the lamp shades, the flowered wallpaper, the numerous religious pictures in heavy, gold-leafed frames and the various souvenirs arranged with precision on top of each table, and she wondered what a real interior decorator would think of it.

Then, hating herself for such treachery, she said, "How've you been, Aunt Rosa?"

"We had a little excitement the other night. Anna won at bingo, but she'll tell you all about it herself."

"I haven't gotten over to see you because I've been staying in the city, working on a case."

Aunt Rosa nodded. "Frank told us all about it. You be careful, Teresa."

Terry thought of mentioning Cindi, then decided not to ruin the day. Instead, they talked about how the neighborhood was running down, how the prices of everything were going up, and the Mets' chances at the pennant.

With a gesture that was second nature to her, Aunt Rosa had taken the tarot cards from the table beside her and was now shuffling them over and over as she talked. Terry knew she was dying to give her a reading, so she finally said, "Going to read the cards for me today?"

"If you like, Teresa."

Terry nodded, and Aunt Rosa moved a snack tray over in front of her and began to spread out the cards. Aunt Rosa got to the usual part about the man in Terry's future—there was always a man in any unmarried woman's future when she read the cards—but then she said something that startled Terry.

"The man is in clothing."

"You mean he's not naked?" asked Terry.

She got a reproving look. "Of course he's not naked. I think what it means is his work has something to do with clothing."

It had to be a coincidence, thought Terry, but she just gestured for her aunt to go on.

The second shock came when her aunt said, "I keep seeing this man, but I also see lies. Somebody's telling lies."

That line might have given Terry a heart attack until she remembered Kathy and her big mouth and the well-known family grapevine.

"How can you reconcile tarot cards with church dogma?" she asked her aunt, who was the only one in the family who received daily communion.

"There's no church law against tarot cards."

"Fortune-telling isn't exactly approved of."

"I'm not telling your fortune, Teresa. I'm merely reading the cards. Nobody says they're to be taken seriously."

Terry remembered taking them very seriously as a child, but then that was no doubt due to the fact that her aunt always told her everything she wanted to hear.

That made her wonder if she wanted to hear about a man in clothing. "Are you psychic?" she asked Aunt Rosa. That was a question that had never crossed her mind before.

Aunt Rosa's usually cheerful countenance turned serious. "I think I might be, Teresa. I know right now you're troubled about your father, but I don't know why. All I can tell you is that everything will work out for the best."

That again sounded like Kathy, who used the telephone the way other people used air to breathe.

Still, Terry decided that she didn't mind the tarot cards having come up with Wynn. She might not believe in them, but then again, she figured she needed all the help she could get.

That night, when Mike was in bed asleep, she cooked up a pot of spaghetti sauce to take to the city with her the next day. She wanted Wynn to know what real Italian spaghetti tasted like, but she also wanted to be able to fix it for him in a hurry. This way she'd only have to boil the pasta and dinner would be all set to serve.

A little self-examination told her that she was trying to impress him with her cooking since she didn't feel able to compete with all the models he knew as far as looks went. At the same time, she knew that she didn't want to be liked for her looks or her cooking; she wanted to be liked for herself, which was a big problem when she was pretending to be someone else whenever she saw him.

Before going to bed she gave Kathy a call. "Well, what did you think?" she asked as soon as her sister answered.

"I think Pop needs a shrink."

"Was she just thrilled to meet you?" Terry asked.

"Thrilled to pieces. Went crazy over the kids. I wonder how she'd feel if they started calling her Grandma."

"What did Johnny think?"

There was a significant pause, then Kathy said, "I'd rather not discuss it."

"Come on, Kath, what happened?"

"He thought she was sexy."

"You're kidding!"

"I swear to you, Terry, he made at least three thinly veiled remarks about her body on the way home."

"Well, I guess Pop finds her sexy."

"Pop is definitely off his rocker."

"By the way, Kath, you didn't happen to mention Wynn Ransome to the aunts, did you?"

"What for? They wouldn't know who he was."

"I'm serious. You sure you didn't say anything?"

"Not that I can remember, but I don't think so. Why?"

Terry told her about the tarot cards.

Kathy said, "I don't know, maybe I did and I don't remember it. Either that or Aunt Rosa's better at it than we thought. Maybe I ought to get a reading, find out what Johnny's up to."

"Haven't you talked to him yet?"

"No, I haven't. But I called a private detective. You know what those guys charge?"

Terry didn't, but she was curious.

"Two hundred bucks a day plus expenses, that's what."

That didn't sound like a bad option if she ever wanted to quit the force, Terry thought. "Did you hire one?"

"No. I was going to beg you one more time. Please, Terry, just follow him one night after work—that's all I'm asking."

"I couldn't even if I wanted to. I go to Le Club every night now. I'll talk to him, though, if you want."

"What for, so he can lie to you? Even if he tells you the truth, you'll just lie to me."

"I promise I'll tell you the truth."

Terry said she'd call Johnny at work the next day, then ended up telling Kathy that Wynn was coming to her place for dinner the next night.

"I can't believe someone in our family is dating a celebrity," said Kathy, a wistful note in her voice.

"I wouldn't exactly call it dating."

"I would. I just hope you don't blow it, Terry. I'd sure like to meet him in person sometime."

Terry thought about that while she was getting ready for bed. She thought about Wynn meeting her family. She thought of him meeting her son, who didn't think mothers should date. She thought of her father and his young girlfriend, of Kathy and her big mouth, of her brother and his wife and their constant fighting. She even thought of Aunt Rosa telling his fortune.

Spelled out like that, her family sounded as if it came straight out of a soap opera—a daytime soap, unfortunately, not one of the ones at night that were filled with rich, glamorous people.

She had a sneaking suspicion that Wynn was not the type to fit in.

Chapter Five

Monday had its good and its bad periods, one of the bad ones being when Terry called Johnny at work. She put it off, procrastinating until almost noon, but she had promised Kathy and she always kept her promises.

Still, she felt awfully foolish saying to Johnny, "Listen, my sister thinks you're cheating on her."

She waited for his laugh, but instead, after a tense silence, he said, "Your sister's crazy, you know that?" and then hung up on her.

Terry was left with a bad taste in her mouth. Hanging up on her had been the same as telling her it was none of her business, and of course, it wasn't. Nor did she believe Johnny was doing any such thing, but once Kathy got something in her mind she wouldn't let go of it.

Thoroughly chastened, she called Kathy and reported the conversation, but Kathy still didn't see it her way. "That sure sounds guilty, don't you think? Hanging up on you like that?"

"No, Kath, I don't. I think he was trying to tell me not to butt into other people's business." And he was right. She had probably messed up all the good feelings she and Johnny had always had toward each other.

The best thing that came out of the day happened in the midst of a discussion with the lieutenant and Kyle. They were talking about having Le Club come up with a roster of members who worked out every night, when something else occurred to Terry.

"Maybe it's an employee," she said, which resulted in both men looking at her with respect—renewed on the part of Lieutenant Corbet, new on the part of Kyle.

"We should've thought of that before," said the lieutenant. "It makes sense, someone who's there every night."

"And it'll mean a lot fewer having to be checked out," added Kyle.

A bad moment came a few minutes later when, knowing it had to be done, she said, "By the way, I'm having Wynn Ransome over to dinner tonight."

So much for their looking at her with respect. Lieutenant Corbet was looking doubtful and Kyle was looking outraged.

It was Lieutenant Corbet who spoke first. "Did he invite himself over?"

"No. I invited him."

"Damn it, can't you leave off dating until after we've solved the case?" Kyle complained.

"I don't see what difference it makes," said Terry. "I've tried flirting, but he's the only one who pays any attention to me. Anyway, he's nice."

"Well," said Lieutenant Corbet, "I never really saw him as a suspect, but I guess we can't take any chances. You'll be over there before they arrive, Kyle, and—"

Terry broke in. "Over where?"

Lieutenant Corbet's brows moved toward the ceiling, which was not a good sign. "You weren't contemplating an evening alone with a possible suspect, were you, Terry?"

Terry didn't have the guts to argue.

"I thought not," continued the lieutenant. "I think the closet in the entry hall, Kyle—as I recall it was adequately roomy."

Kyle was looking about as pleased at having to spend time in Terry's closet as she was at having to have him there. She wished now she'd never invited Wynn over. A threesome with Kyle was not her idea of a great way to spend an evening.

Moroni was sent over to Le Club to get copies of all the employees' applications, then Terry and Kyle spent the rest of the day feeding the names into the computers. By the time they left work, they had gotten partial feedback on some of the names, but none came up sounding like Jack the Ripper.

Pop called just before Terry left to go home. Since he generally didn't bother her at work unless it was some kind of emergency, she couldn't figure out why all he appeared to be doing was passing the time of day, even becoming mundane as he mentioned the weather.

"Is there anything wrong, Pop?" she finally asked.

"Not a thing. Can't I even call my daughter to say hello?"

That sounded suspiciously unlike him. "Mike okay?"

"Your son is fine."

"Well, then I'll talk to you later, okay?"

Pop, his voice sounding sneaky, said, "Cindi said to say hello."

So that's what it was all about. Terry should have realized it sooner. Pop wanted to sound her out on Cindi, but wouldn't come right out and say so.

"Tell her hello for me," said Terry, refusing to be drawn into a discussion of Pop's little Lolita.

Pop seemed to be waiting for more, but when it wasn't forthcoming he finally hung up.

She was damned if she was going to condone that misguided romance. She wished now she hadn't been so critical of the widow Minotti, who at least, to her credit, had been over forty. Still, the widow had been a nag, there was no getting around it. And why a good-looking, charming man like Terry's father couldn't find someone his equal, she didn't know.

Terry wasn't looking forward much to that night. It wasn't that she didn't want to see Wynn; in fact, she found she had been spending half her time lately thinking about him. But it seemed, in retrospect, that perhaps she shouldn't have invited him over. It sounded like the kind of thing a woman did when she was trying to snare a man—give him a home-cooked meal and all that. She knew that when she invited him she had had no such thought in mind; it was more just plain showing off, showing him that she could cook better than whoever did the cooking at that famous place he took her to. But she was awfully afraid he wouldn't see it that way. And why should he?

Then there was the matter of Kyle in the closet. That part sounded like nothing so much as a French farce.

The woman, the man and the extra man in the closet. As it was she had trouble enough talking to Wynn, what with all the lying she had to do. But to talk to him with even the least semblance of normalcy, knowing that Kyle was listening in the closet—just thinking about it was enough to give her an ulcer.

In order to prolong the time before they got to her sublet, and also, in a perverse way, to prolong the time Kyle would have to spend waiting in the closet—because he was bypassing Le Club and going directly there—she took along her new bathing suit, thinking she could get in some more practice on the new stroke Wynn had taught her. And just maybe he'd teach her another.

She saw Lisa in the locker room and talked her into running around the track with her instead of using the cycles, which were at least twice as boring. She told Lisa about the whole thing—about Wynn coming over to dinner and about Kyle having to hide in the closet—and Lisa started laughing so hard they both finally had to stop on the edge of the track because their sides were aching.

"I'd give anything to be in that closet, too," Lisa said when she was able to stop laughing long enough.

"Be my guest," Terry told her, but she was only kidding. She didn't think Kyle or Lieutenant Corbet would appreciate her having confided to Lisa who she was.

"This Kyle, is he cute?" Lisa asked.

"Forget it. The last thing you want to date is a cop."

"I don't know. Cops have a certain appeal."

"That's television cops. In person, forget it. They're the worst bunch of chauvinist pigs in the world." Although to be fair, there were exceptions—Lieutenant Corbet, for one.

Lisa had also brought a swimsuit, and when they got to the pool and Wynn was there, Terry introduced them. She wouldn't have known Lisa was the same woman who had been nearly swooning over Wynn that first night. Lisa just shook his hand and said hi, not coming on to him at all, which Terry appreciated.

Wynn looked at Terry's new swimsuit in a mocking way and said, "Ralph Lauren."

She said, "What?" and then he and Lisa started to laugh.

"She really isn't interested in clothes," Lisa said to him.

"I know," he said, and then they both explained to Terry that Ralph Lauren was Wynn's biggest competitor.

Wynn showed Terry a new stroke where she swam on her back and her legs moved like frogs' legs. It was so easy she loved it, but the only problem was that she couldn't see where she was going and kept banging her head on the sides of the pool.

She was feeling relaxed and good by the time she and Wynn left Le Club, but during the walk over to her place she started to get nervous. She thought Wynn sensed it and guessed that he probably thought it had to do with the cooking. She kept thinking of Kyle in the closet. She would have given anything to be able to tell Wynn about it, but of course she didn't. Not that she thought it mattered—if she thought Wynn was the strangler, she sure wouldn't have been cooking for him.

When they got to her place she put the key in the door. Wynn, looking around, said, "Is this a hotel?"

"A residential hotel," she told him.

He looked kind of curious at that, so she said, "I like the conveniences of a hotel," which added one more to the long string of lies she had already told him. Not that she didn't really appreciate the conveniences, but it sounded as though she always lived in hotels when, in fact, the only hotel she'd ever been in previously was one in Atlantic City when she was on her honeymoon.

She didn't know what he had been expecting, but he looked pretty impressed when they got inside. He said, "I guess you really are an interior decorator," but she was thinking of Kyle and wasn't paying any attention, so he had to repeat it.

"What'd you think I was?" she asked him.

"I don't know, Terry. It's not that I thought you were lying about it, but you just didn't strike me as one."

"Why? What's an interior decorator like?"

He started to smile. "Well, the only one I know is mine, and he's gay."

For some reason she took that wrong and said, "For that matter, I would've figured all dress designers were gay." She was instantly sorry when she saw the expression on his face.

"Are you implying it's not a masculine profession?"

Instead of keeping her big mouth shut, she said, "Well, it's not exactly like digging ditches."

"No. For one thing, it pays better."

Partly because she felt they were getting the evening off to a bad start, and partly because she knew Kyle was probably doubled up with laughter at this point, she said, "Sorry. That was pretty rude of me. Would you like a drink?"

He had a rueful smile on his face when he said, "I guess I asked for it. Yes, I'd love a drink."

"All I have is beer and wine."

"A beer would be great."

She didn't know whether he really meant it or whether he was trying to act like a ditch digger, but she didn't question it. She got them each a beer, then decided to foil Kyle for the moment and took Wynn out into the garden.

It was hot and muggy outside but there was a slight breeze in the garden and the buildings surrounding it provided shade. "This is really nice," Wynn said, looking around.

"Make yourself at home," she said. Then she excused herself and put the pasta on to boil and the sauce in the pan to warm.

It suddenly hit her that this was the first time she had cooked for a man since her husband died. There were Pop and Mike, of course, but they didn't count. It seemed strange, as though she were playing house but in someone else's kitchen. It began to make her feel uncomfortable until she remembered Kyle in the closet, and that brought her back to normal.

When she joined Wynn in the yard he was sitting at the table, his legs stretched out in front of him and his head tilted back to catch the breeze. She knew they would be more comfortable in the air-conditioned apartment but was hoping to have some time alone with him without benefit of Kyle's ears.

He interrupted her thoughts by saying, "How'd you get into interior decorating?"

Thinking fast, she said, "By accident, really. Friends saw my place and wanted me to do theirs, and that led to doing it full time. What about you? How'd you get in dress designing?"

"Actually, rather like you," he said. "Friends admired the dresses I made for myself and—"

"Very funny."

He must have thought it was, because he started laughing.

"Do you enjoy it?" she asked, still not understanding what he could possibly get out of it—except money and fame, of course.

"You're determined to see it as some useless profession, aren't you? Because you don't like clothes, no one should."

"Where's the excitement in it?" she pressed on, really wanting to know.

He took a long drink of his beer, looking as if he were trying to decide whether to give her a straight answer. "The excitement is in designing something that works, that women like and that sells well. Where's the excitement in decorating apartments?"

That was a good question, but it had her stumped. But oh, how she longed to be able to tell him about police work. "The excitement," she finally said, "is in turning a dingy New York apartment into something livable."

"Not a bad answer," he said.

"Thank you," she said, getting up and taking a bow. "And now, if you'll excuse me for a moment, I'll put dinner on the table."

"Can we eat out here?"

"Great idea," she said, thinking that Kyle could sit in that closet and sweat to death while he wondered what was going on outside.

But in the middle of her perfectly marvelous meal, it suddenly started to rain, and they had to run inside carrying their drowning plates of spaghetti.

"It looks ruined," Terry said, surveying the spaghetti, now swimming in rainwater.

"Don't worry about it. The first half, anyway, was maybe the best spaghetti I've ever had."

"Thanks, but are you any judge of spaghetti?"

"I take it you didn't like it at Elaine's."

"The worst," she told him.

"Yes, but you don't go there for the food. You go to be seen."

"You mean it's worth bad food to be seen?"

"I hadn't thought about it, but I guess not."

"And were we seen?"

He nodded. "Indeed we were."

"Does that mean all the 'in' people will be asking me to decorate their apartments?"

His eyes narrowed, making the slant more noticeable. "Can we call a truce, or is this going to go on indefinitely?"

"Is what going to go on?" she said, trying to play the innocent.

"You obviously don't approve of either my profession or my life-style. Why, then, did you cook dinner for me? Was it just to prove a point?"

She guessed it had been to prove a point, but she didn't want to admit it. "Okay," she said, "a truce. What do you want to talk about, the Mets' chances?"

He didn't, unfortunately, nor did she wish to discuss the latest Broadway hit. He tried—in fact, they both tried, but they couldn't seem to come up with a topic of conversation they could agree on. But despite that, he didn't appear to be bored. He had, instead, a hopeful, waiting look about him.

Let's face it, she told herself, *maybe he's just waiting to strangle me. Or get me in bed.* But she had a strong feeling it wasn't either.

Then what the hell was it?

FOR THE LIFE OF HIM, Wynn couldn't figure her out. For one thing, her apartment just didn't fit. It was beautifully decorated—if you liked art deco, which he didn't except maybe in Soho restaurants. It was just that most of it didn't look lived in. Granted, he hadn't seen the bedroom, and the kitchen looked well used. But the living room didn't reflect her personality in any way. There were no books, no magazines and no newspapers. There was a cunningly contrived desk, but it lacked the usual bills or papers or whatnot that a desk usually drew like a magnet. The only personal thing in the entire room was a picture of a child, a girl of perhaps two, framed in an expensive silver frame atop the desk. But when he asked her who the child was, it took her too long to answer. She finally said it was a friend's child. Except no one bought an expensive frame for a photo of a friend's child, at least not in his experience.

She also didn't seem at ease in the apartment. Of course, that could very easily have been because of his presence, only he had a feeling it wasn't entirely that. At times, and this was really preposterous, she appeared to be acting as though she were in a TV show. Not actressy, nothing like that. More as if a camera was on her. None of it made any sense at all, and it could be he was imagining it.

The only thing he knew about her that he would swear to was that she was a damn fine cook—if, in fact, she had cooked the meat sauce herself, and he had no reason to doubt it. She also had a healthy appetite, which was a novelty after dating models. They tended to either nibble on salads or eat hearty meals and then excuse themselves to go to the ladies' room, where, he had heard, they promptly forced the meal back up so as not to put on any weight. He thought that practice was pretty sick, but on the other hand, he knew just what models had to contend with. And the biggest thing they had to contend with was added pounds. Still, he had never considered models good dinner companions.

There seemed to be no meeting ground between them; they didn't have the same interests. He'd tried his best to come up with an agreeable subject of conversation, but nothing jelled. He wondered why he was even wasting his time and then he admitted that there was no one else he would rather be with at the moment. And he thought that if he kept seeing her, eventually they'd start acting natural toward each other, which wasn't the case now. He thought it was worth a little time, anyway.

The only really good discussion they had had was when he mentioned the stranglings. He had said, "I see you're not going to be frightened out of working out by those newspaper stories."

She became more animated as soon as he said it.

"No, but did you notice how the women's attendance has dropped off?"

"I couldn't help noticing. You and your friend Lisa were two of the few blondes there tonight. You don't think maybe you ought to quit for the duration?"

"What for? You're the only man there who talks to me, and I don't think—"

She broke off then, and he finished the sentence for her. "And you don't think I'm the strangler? Is that what you were going to say?"

She nodded, looking embarrassed.

"You're right, I'm not. But I don't know how you could be really sure of that."

Her eyes had a gleam in them when she said, "Well, I figure if you like women enough to design clothes for them, you wouldn't want to kill off potential customers."

"And yet somehow I don't see you as a potential customer."

She smiled. "But you can't be sure of that."

"Nor can you be sure I'm not dying to strangle you."

"Well, my muscles are building up from those machines, so you're going to have a fight on your hands if you try."

"I'll keep that in mind," he said, wondering if that was a warning not to get physical with her.

"Why do you suppose he does it, Wynn?"

"I'd say he was a nut."

"But what kind of a nut? Why blondes?"

"I'm not really up on criminal psychology, but what comes to mind would be some blonde who had done him wrong in some way, I suppose. It certainly isn't one of those mother complexes or he wouldn't be going after young women."

"Young professional women."

"Sure. But that could be because that's mostly what you get at Le Club. If he worked out on the West Side, he'd probably be killing young actresses or dancers."

"I hadn't thought of that."

"For what it's worth, I wish you would quit going until he's caught. You're going to be a perfect target if you're one of the few blondes there."

"I'll be careful."

"Sure, but I imagine most women in New York are careful, as a matter of course. And the guy must be credible or they wouldn't have invited him in."

"Maybe they invited him over for a spaghetti dinner."

"It's not a joking matter, Terry."

"I know. I just couldn't resist that."

He knew women well enough to know that even though she had invited him to dinner, she hadn't had anything further in mind. He wasn't about to rush things, either. Anyway, although sex was certainly an icebreaker, he liked to have a handle on whom he was going to bed with. And she was still too unknown. He preferred reality in bed to fantasy.

Still, the physical attraction was strong enough that when he was leaving and she was walking him to the door, he turned and was about to give her a good-night kiss. Suddenly she seemed instinctively to move away from him, banging her shoulder against the closet door in the process.

She was rubbing her shoulder and he said, "Are you all right?"

"I'm fine."

"You'd think I was trying to strangle you."

For some reason she seemed to be trying not to laugh. "I'm sorry. I guess I overreacted."

"It wasn't an attack, Terry. I was just going to kiss you good-night, which in polite society is a way of thanking the hostess for a delicious meal."

"You could try again," she said, looking up at him with twitching lips. Twitching from withheld laughter, of course, not passion.

He waited a beat, then held out his arms and she came into them. But now he could feel the laughter shaking her body so he just looked at her, and after a while she said, "Well?"

"As soon as you can get the laughter under control."

"I'm sorry. I really don't know why I'm laughing. Look, would you mind, could we go outside and kiss?"

"It's raining outside."

"You mind the rain?"

"Not at all. If you think it's romantic kissing in the rain, then by all means let's give it a try."

She didn't say anything to that, just opened the door, and they went outside. Then, without his even making a move, she went into his arms and lifted her face, and surprisingly, it was romantic kissing in the rain. It was also wet, of course, but it was a light summer rain and not at all uncomfortable.

"Thank you," she said, when he at last broke it off.

"What for?"

"For not minding kissing me outside."

"Listen, if you like the water, I'll kiss you in the pool next time."

She laughed. "You must think I'm crazy."

"No. Different, maybe, but not crazy."

"Well, I guess I'll see you on Wednesday."

"Terry, listen to me. I think I'm going to walk you home from now on."

"That's not necessary, Wynn."

"It is for my peace of mind. You might be developing muscles, but you're not all that big."

She straightened up, making herself a good inch taller. "If I'm going home after working out, you're welcome to walk with me," she said, and they left it at that.

Her statement made him wonder if she was seeing anyone else. But he didn't think so. It was his experience that women who were dating never failed to bring it up. And she had even said he was the only man at Le Club who talked to her, which was something most women would never have admitted to.

She was different all right. Maybe too different. He certainly didn't get the feeling he was getting to know her.

KYLE CAME OUT of the closet singing, "I'm kissing in the rain," and Terry felt like punching him in the mouth.

"You couldn't have cut the evening a little shorter?" he asked.

"It's not even eleven, Kyle. Are your dates that short?"

"They'd be shorter if I had someone waiting for hours in an uncomfortable, hot closet."

"How come you didn't jump out and protect me when I slammed into the closet door?"

"Because it sounded like he needed more protecting than you did. If he's the strangler, all I've got to say is he's sure slow about it."

"He's not the strangler. I never for a minute thought he was."

"Then you're wasting your time seeing him."

"I don't consider it a waste of time."

"Come on, Terry. You can do all the dating you want when the case is closed."

"I work all day and now I have to go to Le Club every night. I would think I'd get some time for my private life."

"You do—you get weekends. Got any more of that terrific spaghetti left?"

"Why?"

"Have a heart, Caputo. I've been in a closet while you've been out here eating and drinking and having a great time."

She relented and went to the kitchen and reheated what was left.

"What do you see in that guy, anyway?" Kyle said. He followed her and was making himself at home.

"Why? What's wrong with him?"

"Come on, a dress designer?"

"What's wrong with that?"

"Don't give me a hard time. I heard you saying the same thing to him."

"He's nice. I like him."

"I think it's probably more that he's good-looking and rich."

"I didn't even know who he was when I met him."

"But you found out fast enough, didn't you?"

"Kyle," she said, slamming a plate of spaghetti down on the table, "just eat and shut up. I think I prefer you in the closet."

The next day, though, the lieutenant agreed with Kyle. "You're going to have to knock off the dating for the duration, Terry. No guy's going to move in on you if he thinks you're close with someone else. Especially if that someone else is always around."

"I've seen him exactly twice, Lieutenant. That's hardly always around."

"Terry, don't think I don't understand. But you're there for decoy work, and dating the wrong guy is just undermining that work. You say there aren't many blondes left working out—well, this could be your chance."

"Then I wish you'd let me level with him."

"Not yet. But if you want to do some investigating on your own, maybe put him somewhere else at the time of one of the killings, I might change my mind."

"And how am I supposed to do that?"

"I'll be damned if I know," admitted the lieutenant.

"I'LL BE DAMNED if I know," Meg was saying.

"Are you telling me there's not one model in New York City who looks like what I want?"

"That's what I said."

Wynn sighed with exasperation. "Then go out on the streets and find one."

"Who is it you're drawing? Is that a real person or just someone you made up?" Meg asked.

"Real. But she's not a model."

"But at least you know who she is. You really expect me to start walking the streets to find some perfect type you're looking for?"

"I suppose not."

"Who is she, anyway, Wynn?"

"A woman who works out at Le Club. An interior decorator."

"She'd probably be thrilled to model for you."

Somehow he didn't think so.

"YOU WANT TO GET something to eat?" Wynn asked Terry on Wednesday night, determined to walk her home.

Terry had been following instructions and avoiding him all night, but he caught up with her when she was leaving.

"Thanks, but I've got to get home," she told him, avoiding his eyes.

"You have to eat, don't you?"

She looked around, didn't see Kyle lurking anywhere, and decided a quick meal wouldn't hurt. "Couldn't we just stop at a Burger King?"

"You eat that junk?"

"I like Burger King."

He gave in, but when they were seated and eating their burgers, he said, "I don't know how someone who cooks as well as you do could eat this."

"Be honest. It's not that bad."

He ignored that. "I've got something I want to show you," he said, picking up the briefcase he'd been carrying that night and setting it on the table. He opened it, took out a couple of drawings, and handed them to her.

It took her a moment to look from the clothes to the person wearing them, and then she realized what he had done. "That looks like me," she said, not sure she liked his drawing pictures of her. "Except that the hair is dark and short."

"I like the way you look in my clothes."

"If anyone else said that, it would sound pretty strange." She was trying to make a joke of it, but was flattered that he spent his time drawing her picture.

"I think you're the right type."

"I imagine a model would look better in them. Aren't you supposed to be tall to wear clothes well?"

"That's always been the reasoning, but I don't see why. My stuff isn't high fashion—it's supposed to be for the average woman."

"And you see me as the average woman?" Terry was not pleased, but she saw the logic in it.

"I see you as normal. I see you as someone who doesn't think she has to starve herself to death to look good."

After that remark, she wished she hadn't ordered two burgers. "Why'd you make my hair short? And dark?"

"I don't know. I just liked the look with my clothes, I guess."

That was a polite way of telling her she didn't make it as a blonde, since he was too much of a gentleman to ask her if she bleached her hair.

She figured the discussion was over and went back to eating, so she almost choked on her food when he said, "Would you be interested in modeling?"

"You've got to be kidding!"

But she could tell he wasn't because he was looking serious and businesslike. "Just for me. Just for a special promotion I want to do."

"Sorry, it just doesn't interest me."

"It'd pay well."

She stared him down and he finally said, "Okay, so you don't need the money."

That was a real laugh. She always needed money. "I just can't imagine a more boring way of earning money," she told him.

"Unlike the thrills of interior decorating, right?"

"At least I don't have to worry about how I look when I'm doing that."

"You wouldn't have to worry if you worked for me. You already look exactly right."

He was not an easy man to dissuade. "Find someone else."

"I tried. None of the models look like you."

"Wynn, open your eyes. I'm a type you see all over the city. I could find you ten women in an hour who'd do just as well." Hell, she could find half a dozen in her own family.

He smiled, and she could tell he was going to try another tack. He did. "I thought it would be fun working with you," he said, putting the drawings away and closing his briefcase.

"I'm sorry, Wynn, but even if it appealed to me, I'm busy on a big job right now."

"Some socialite's apartment?"

"No, a hotel." That seemed to impress him, and she was feeling pretty smart until she realized it was just one more lie she'd have to account for later—if there was a later, at the rate they were going.

Then she wondered what he'd think if he knew he was trying to get a cop to model for him. She imagined it would be a first on Seventh Avenue, at any rate.

"Think about it anyway, won't you? It could wait until your job's done."

"That'll just hold you up. I'm telling you, Wynn, you can find someone who'll do just as well."

"You won't let me make you rich and famous, huh?"

"So I can be recognized at Elaine's?"

"All right, forget I mentioned it."

He sounded a little annoyed with her, which didn't make it the greatest time to tell him she couldn't see him for a while. On the other hand, it might come as a great relief to him.

She had been trying for two days to come up with a reason to give him. When she couldn't she decided to improvise when the time came.

Well, the time was now and she still couldn't come up with anything. If she gave him some lame reason, she knew she'd never see him again.

In the end, she didn't say anything.

Chapter Six

"You want to hear something funny, Kath?"

"I could use a laugh," said her sister, sounding unusually serious.

"Wynn wants me to model his clothes in advertisements. Says he'll make me rich and famous."

She waited for the expected laughter, but it didn't come. Instead, faintly at first and then more loudly, she heard what sounded like crying.

"Kathy? You okay?"

More crying, sobbing now, and then her sister's voice, "No, I'm not okay."

"What's the matter? What happened?"

There was more sobbing before Kathy got herself under control. "What do you think happened? I was right, that's what."

"If you're talking about Johnny, I don't believe it."

"It's true, Terry. I got a baby-sitter today, and then I went down to where Johnny works and I followed him when he got off. And let me tell you, it's not easy following someone in a subway without being seen."

"So what happened?"

"I'll tell you what happened. He went straight to this house, and a woman opened the door and let him in."

"Uh, Kath, that could've meant anything," said Terry, although she was having doubts for the first time.

"I waited, Terry, and he didn't come back out. And it's ten o'clock and he still isn't home."

"Maybe he saw you," said Terry. "Maybe he knew what you were up to and went there on purpose."

"Do you really believe that?"

"No. But it's hard to believe Johnny would do something like that."

"I'm confronting him when he comes home. But I wanted to let you know."

"Don't do anything rash, will you?"

"Rash? Like what, throw him out? You're damn right I'm going to do something rash."

"Sleep on it, at least."

"If Nick had run around on you, would you just have taken it?"

Terry, who had never admitted it to anyone, said, "I think he was, Kath, and I did."

"But you weren't sure."

"I was pretty sure. Sometimes at night, when he thought I was sleeping, he'd get up and go into the living room and make phone calls. I could hear him—he'd be whispering."

"And you didn't confront him with it?"

"I guess I was scared to. I loved him so much and I was afraid of losing him. I wasn't very brave in those days, Kath."

"So what finally happened?"

"He got killed."

"Oh, Terry, I'm so sorry. I wish you'd told me about it at the time."

"It's okay, I've been over it a long time. And once he was dead it didn't seem to matter. I was just glad that maybe he got some extra happiness since he had to die so young."

"Well, I'm not quite as saintly as you. If Johnny's going to get some extra happiness, it's not going to be while he's living here."

"I'm not a saint," Terry said. "I've grown up since then. It's just that I'm not sure it's worth breaking up a family over." That was a lie; if Nick were around now and cheating on her, she'd throw him out in an instant. It was just that Kathy had never had to support herself, and Terry didn't know how she'd manage with three kids. Still, that was no reason to forgive him.

"Listen, Kath—be calm when you talk to him, and don't lose your temper. And call me right away and let me know what happens, okay?"

"That's a little hard when you won't give me your phone number."

"I'll give it to you, but don't use it again after tonight, promise?"

But Kathy didn't call that night, and it wasn't until the next day that Terry learned what had happened. Surprisingly, she heard it from Johnny, not Kathy.

She was in the office when his call came, and the first thing he said was, "I'm sorry I hung up on you the other day, Terry."

"I don't blame you, Johnny. It was none of my business. I don't know why I let Kathy get me into those things."

"The thing is, she was right."

Terry sat for a moment in shocked silence. "Oh, Johnny, I'm really sorry to hear that."

"It just got to be too much, Terry. I've been married since I was nineteen. We've got three kids who are always screaming at me for something when I get home. And you know your sister, she never lets up for a minute. I met this woman and she's so different. So quiet. Never asks me for anything."

"Are you in love with her, Johnny?"

"I think so. All I know is I feel really good when I'm around her."

"So what happened last night?"

"Yeah, she said she told you. She kicked me out, Terry. In the middle of the night. I had to go to the Y and get a room. I couldn't go to my folks, you know—not with Mom's heart the way it is."

"So what's going to happen?"

"I don't know. I don't blame her, you understand. I didn't figure on breaking up the marriage, though."

Terry sighed. "Well, the best way to break up a marriage, Johnny, is to cheat on your wife."

"I know I deserve that, Terry, but it's not like I was looking for it. I just happened to meet her; it wasn't anything planned. Anyway, I just wanted you to know I was sorry about hanging up on you. That call of yours really came as a shock, though."

Not any more of a shock than her sister's troubles were to her.

Terry couldn't stop thinking about it the rest of the day. Something like that always shook any faith she might have in men. Were any of them ever faithful? Were they inherently different from women? She knew of no women in her family who had ever cheated on their men, but she wouldn't swear that any of the men had been that faithful.

Not that her sister couldn't be hard to take. Since Kathy was the eldest, her natural bossiness had grown when their mother had died and she had a lot of responsibility thrust on her. Terry had mostly ignored Kathy when she was being bossy, but Tony had suffered from having two older sisters to boss him around. And from the day that Kathy married Johnny, she had changed from a flirtatious minx to a bossy wife—even the advent of three children to boss around hadn't appeared to lessen Johnny's share.

Terry thought the problem was that the women in her family were stronger than the men. If Johnny had stood up to Kathy, refused to let her take control, her sister would have been much happier.

It had affected Tony, too. Instead of finding a different kind of woman to marry, he had ended up with Joanna. Joanna wasn't bossy and didn't nag, but she was a lot stronger than Tony, and probably a lot smarter, too. In fact, much as Terry loved Tony, she often wondered what Joanna had seen in him. Granted, he was good-looking and charming, but she would have thought Joanna would want more than that.

All of this might, of course, explain Pop and the nymphet, but she really didn't want to think about that.

Terry was depressed when she got to Le Club that night. She wished it weren't a Tuesday, when neither Lisa nor Wynn would be around to talk to.

She tried to concentrate on working out, on forgetting about Kathy and Johnny for a while, and because of this she wasn't even aware at first that a man was watching her, checking her out.

When she did finally catch his eye, he smiled at her, and she automatically smiled back.

He was, of course, good-looking. They were all good-looking. This one had black curly hair and dark eyes, too reminiscent of the men in her family to really interest her.

He was following her through the circuit, always one machine behind her, always finishing before she did and standing and watching her while she completed her reps.

It made her self-conscious, made her strain harder than she would have normally. She was aware of the sweat on her face, although she no longer perspired nearly as much as she had in the beginning. She tried to keep a cool expression on her face, as though she weren't aware that he was watching every move she made. Unlike Wynn, though, this one struck her as someone who could be the strangler.

He didn't look like a homicidal maniac, it wasn't that—although the strangler no doubt didn't, either—he was just very watchful, much more so than was warranted. She knew most of the other women at Le Club would have said something to him, made a joke of it, maybe even flirted with him. She tried to think of something to say to break the mood, that watchfulness, but her mind was a blank.

Then, just when the tension was finally getting to the point where she was about ready to skip the rest of the machines just to avoid him, he said, "I haven't seen you here before."

For some reason she wanted to run, but remembering why she was there, she gave him a polite smile and said, "I haven't been coming long."

"How do you like it?"

"It's great."

She vacated the machine and went to the next, and he took her place. She began pulling down the weights with her arms, straining her muscles, trying to concentrate on breathing correctly. He didn't seem to care if he breathed correctly, because he continued talking. "I've been coming about six months. Before that I worked out at La Lanne's, but there's no comparison."

"This is my first health club," Terry told him, not wanting to mention the Y. She didn't want to talk, either, but if he was the one, she didn't want him to get away.

"You look in good shape," he said, his eyes on her legs. That wasn't the kind of thing usually said to you at Le Club.

"I'm working on it," she told him.

"My name's Craig."

"Terry."

After that he didn't say any more and she was half hoping he had lost interest. She could see that Kyle had noticed the interplay and was looking over at them with interest.

When she got to the last machine, though, he started up again. "Want to get a drink after?" he asked her.

She didn't. What she wanted to get was some food, but she arranged her face in what she hoped was the appropriate display of interest and said, "Sure. But I've only got time for one."

And then he'd walk her home, and then he'd lure her inside, and then.:... Like hell he would!

When she was finished, she signaled to Kyle to follow her to the elevator. They managed to get one to themselves and she said, "I'm going for a drink with him."

"I noticed he came on to you pretty strong."

"Yeah, well, that doesn't mean much. This *is* supposed to be the big singles place, you know."

"Did you get any feeling about him?"

"Nothing good. But that's probably just paranoia. I automatically suspect any good-looking guy who makes a play for me."

"I've made plays for you."

"Knock it off, Kyle. So what do you think?"

Kyle's leer faded. "I think it's the closet for me again."

"Well, head over there soon. I'm only going out for one drink, then I'll say I have to get home."

"If he walks you home, invite him in."

"I'm not going to make it that easy for him. I want to see how persuasive he can be."

CRAIG WAS WAITING for her in the lobby and they walked outside together. "You know this area?" he asked her.

"Fairly well. I don't live too far from here."

"Maybe you know a good bar, then."

Terry took him to a bar just a block from her apartment, a quiet-looking place she passed whenever she went to Le Club. She was expecting him to opt for a secluded booth, but he took a seat at the bar and she took the stool beside him.

"What'll you have?" he asked her.

"Just a beer. Light."

He ordered himself a vodka-and-orange-juice, telling her that beer would only put back on the fat she was working off, which made her feel guilty and endeared him to her even less.

"So what do you do, Terry?"

"I'm an interior decorator."

"Yeah? My sister does that. Well, actually, she has an antique store, but she also fixes up people's places for them. You get many people wanting antiques in the city?"

Not having the slightest idea what people wanted, she said, "Sure, all the time."

"Maybe you could do some business with her. She's on the Cape but comes to the city pretty often."

All of this talk made her relax somewhat. Would a strangler try to drum up business for his sister? On the other hand, he could be lying, just as she was.

She drank her beer, listened to him tell her about corporate finance, and wondered why she found him so boring. Wynn certainly didn't have any more in common with her than Craig, and they were both equally good-looking, but Wynn appealed to her and Craig left her cold.

Unfortunately, she didn't seem to be leaving him cold. He was a toucher—first a hand on her shoulder, then a tap on her arm when he was making a point.

The air-conditioning in the bar was faulty and the beer was making her warm, and she felt that if he touched her one more time she was going to scream.

"I better be getting home," she finally said. "I'm expecting a phone call from one of my clients."

He didn't argue with her, just paid the tab, then took her hand as they were leaving. She left it in place only in the line of duty.

"I'll walk you home," he said, and she didn't demur. She was waiting to see what he'd pull when they got to her door.

He didn't pull anything, though, just stood there and waited for her to get out her keys. Thinking of Kyle in the closet, and the fuss he'd make if she didn't let the guy in, she said, "Would you like to come in for a minute?"

"Sure. I'd like to see your place."

She opened the door and put on the lights, even though it wasn't dark out yet. She saw him looking around, noting every detail.

"What do you think?" she asked him.

"Well, it's not my taste, but it looks good."

So they did have something in common after all.

"All I've got is beer," said Terry, "but if you want one, I think I'm going to have one."

"No, thanks, but I'll have a glass of water if you don't mind."

When Terry got back with the drinks, he was sitting on the couch looking perfectly at home. Wanting to get it over with if he was the strangler so that she would be able to be honest with Wynn, she sat down next to him.

For some reason she wasn't frightened. It could possibly have something to do with the fact that Kyle was in the closet, which meant there was no way anything could really happen to her. She wasn't even on guard when he put his arm across the back of the couch, then moved it down over her shoulders.

"Look, Craig..." she started to say, thinking she shouldn't make it that easy for him. But instead of stopping, he suddenly pulled her to him with a lot more force than she had expected, and was forcing his mouth over hers when she managed to get her arms between them and began shoving at his chest.

"What the hell do you think you're doing?" she asked, furious that he had thought she was that easy.

This just made him smile, as though aroused at the thought of a fight, and he once more tried to kiss her, but this time she moved her head, ramming it against his nose and saying, "Just get your hands off me, will you?"

Craig was holding his nose when Kyle burst out of the closet, for what reason Terry didn't know. But there he was, looking foolish and furious at the same time, and Craig, his nose forgotten, was looking from Kyle to Terry with alarm.

"Listen, buddy, I didn't know she was married," Craig was saying, now taking in the gun in Kyle's hand. "I didn't mean anything, I swear."

Kyle took out his badge and flashed it at him, then began telling him his rights.

"What the hell is this?" Craig kept asking.

"Kyle," said Terry, "I don't think we have any evidence to arrest him on."

Kyle stopped in the middle of his Miranda recitation and looked at her. "Wasn't he trying to strangle you?"

"Christ, are you kidding me?" Craig asked, turning as gray as the couch.

"No, Kyle, he was trying to kiss me."

"Couldn't you have handled that a little better?" Kyle demanded.

"I'm sorry. I didn't think you were going to jump out of the closet so fast."

"Will someone please tell me what's going on?" Craig said.

"We're going to have to take him in, at least until he's cleared," said Kyle. "He knows too much."

"I swear I don't know anything," said Craig, clearly wishing he'd never spoken to Terry in the first place.

Terry could see that he was frightened and said, "We're police officers, Craig. Working under cover on the strangler case."

"And you think I'm the strangler?" He sounded even more amazed than he'd been when Kyle leaped out of the closet.

"Well, I have long blond hair and you were certainly coming on to me."

"That's a crime? I thought you were cute, that's all."

"Look," Kyle said to Craig, "if you can prove you were somewhere else on the nights the women were killed, we'll have to let you go."

"I swear I won't tell anyone who you two are."

"It might help," said Terry, "if you went back to La Lanne's until we catch the guy."

"Hell, after tonight, I think I'd rather go back there anyway. At least the women I met there didn't have guys with guns hiding in their closets."

They took him down to the station, but it didn't take Craig more than twenty minutes to substantiate that he had been in Boston at the time of the last murder.

That news was not only anticlimactic, but in addition Terry felt soiled from having wrestled on the couch with a man she didn't know and didn't like, all in the name of police work.

And after all that, they hadn't even gotten their man.

TRY TO FIGURE WOMEN OUT.

On Wednesday night, Terry acted as though she hardly knew him. He put it down to her probably having had a bad day, although if you wanted to talk about bad days, he'd had to send back 6,000 T-shirts because the dye lot had been bad, which wouldn't endear him to his supplier. On top of that, a water main had burst near his business, temporarily leaving them without electricity and making the streets a disaster area after work. Despite all that, though, he had been looking forward to seeing Terry again, and her sudden indifference was just about the last straw to an already horrendous day.

But the workout relaxed him, eased the tension and put him in a better frame of mind. By the time he was finished he was willing to forgive her, and he hadn't forgotten his promise to walk her home. But when he approached her and asked if she was ready to leave, she just avoided his eyes and said, "You don't need to bother, Wynn. I'm going out with Lisa tonight."

Of course, she was entitled to go out with her friends, and if he'd had any sense at all, he wouldn't have passed on the ticket to the Off-Broadway show someone had tried to give him that day.

He wasn't proud of himself that he hung around the lobby in order to see her leaving with Lisa. He didn't think it was jealousy, only that he wanted to be sure she was safe. And it was while he was hanging around that he noticed something peculiar. There was a muscular guy, not bad-looking in a brutish sort of way, who was following Terry's every move from a corner of the lobby. Of course, Wynn was doing the same thing, but then he felt he had a right to.

And then, right as Lisa caught up with Terry and it became evident that they were leaving together, he saw the guy take one last look at them and then turn around and go back to the elevator bank.

Wynn started to think it was another admirer of hers, and he was trying to figure out whether it bothered him or not when it suddenly occurred to him that the guy could have been the strangler. Maybe he had been staking Terry out but gave up when he saw her leave with Lisa.

Thinking he should at least warn her, and not caring that he might look ridiculous chasing after them, Wynn took off out the door, immediately spotting them about half a block ahead of him. He managed to catch up with them without outright running, and saw the look of surprise Terry gave him.

Lisa was more friendly, saying, "Hi, Wynn, how's it going?"

"I wouldn't bother you, Terry," he said, "but there was a strange man watching you back at the club, and I thought you ought to know."

"You think it might've been the strangler?" asked Lisa. Her eyes widened, but Terry didn't even seem interested.

"I thought he was acting suspiciously," Wynn told them.

"What'd he look like?" Terry asked.

Wynn tried to remember. "I didn't get a good look at his face because he was standing in a dark corner of the lobby, but he looked like a bodybuilder, very muscular."

"What was he wearing?" Terry asked, acting perfectly calm about the whole thing. Hell, maybe she thought he was making it up just to talk to her.

"Jeans and a black T-shirt."

Terry just nodded, and Wynn said, "Well, do me a favor and keep an eye out for him, will you?"

"Sure I will, and thanks," she said, effectively dismissing him.

Well, maybe she wasn't worried, but he sure as hell was going to keep an eye on the man. And if he saw him acting suspiciously again, he just might report his behavior to the police, who, it seemed to him, were doing little or nothing toward solving the case. If he were in charge, he'd have the whole damn club investigated.

"YOU WERE PRETTY RUDE to him," Lisa said.

"I know. But you know who he was talking about, don't you?"

"Sure. Your partner. But he doesn't know that. I think it's nice the way he's worried about you."

"I'm not supposed to be seeing him and I don't know how to get out of it without ruining everything with him."

"You have got a problem."

Terry told her what had occurred the night before without mentioning any name, but she had no sooner finished than Lisa asked, "Was his name Craig?"

"You know him?"

"Several of the women here have had the same experience with him. All you have to do is say hello to the guy and he thinks you're in the bag. Still, you did invite him in. A lot of guys would've seen something in that."

"I know. I was supposed to be leading him on. But I don't feel like going through that many more times."

"I'll bet he died when Kyle shot out of the closet."

Terry started to laugh. "He thought it was my husband."

"I guess those things happen."

No kidding, thought Terry, reminded now of Kathy, and she told Lisa about it.

Lisa said, "It doesn't pay to get involved in family matters, Terry, believe me."

"How do you stay out of them?"

"I manage it by putting a thousand miles between me and my family."

"I couldn't do that—we're pretty close. I'll tell you, though, with my dad and his young girlfriend, and now Kathy and Johnny, if something else happens, that thousand miles doesn't sound like a bad idea."

SHE FIGURED LATER that it had been tempting fate to even say that, because no sooner had she got home and called Mike to check in, when she was told, "There's something you ought to know, Mom."

What next? "Yes, Mike?"

"I'll let him tell you," said Mike, and the next thing she knew her brother, Tony, was on the phone.

"Hey, Terry," he said, sounding full of false cheer. "How's it going with you?"

"What's the problem, Tony?"

"No problem. I just thought I'd pay my nephew a visit."

"Come on, Tony, since when do you pay Mike a visit in the middle of the week? Where's Joanna?"

"Who?"

"Your wife."

"She's home with the kids."

"So what's going on?"

"Listen, Terry, I know you're not one of those women's libbers, so I'll give it to you straight. Joanna got a job."

"That's great. Doing what?"

"I see. You women are going to stick together, is that it?"

"Tony, Joanna had a good job when you married her. I don't see why she shouldn't go back to it if she wants to."

"You know I've been trying to find work. It's just that everyone's laying off."

"I also know you can use the money."

"I got this idea, Terry."

She had heard that before, and it never boded well. "Let me hear it."

"Well, you got this perfectly good boat just sitting here. What I was thinking—with your permission, of course—is that I could take people out charter fishing on it this summer. I'll pay you rent, of course."

"Are you talking about my home, Tony?"

"Yeah, but you don't use it during the day."

"Mike will be off for summer vacation soon."

"He wants to help me. It'll be good for him to have something to do this summer, Terry, be good experience."

"Good of you to think of my son's welfare. But I'm sorry, I don't want a bunch of drunken fishermen in my house all day."

"I swear I won't even let them in the cabin."

Even though she had often let him talk her into one too many schemes when they were kids, she felt herself wavering. "I'll think about it, okay? Come by this weekend and we'll talk it over."

"There's just one thing, Terry."

"What now?"

"I was wondering if I could stay here."

"What're you talking about, Tony?"

"I told Joanna I wasn't coming home until she quit that job."

"I think the whole family's going crazy."

"It's not crazy. What do you think, I'm going to baby-sit while my wife's out working?"

"They're your kids, too, Tony."

"All I'm asking is a favor of my sister. Can I stay here or not? I got one of those futon mattresses I can put on the deck. I won't be any bother."

He was a grown man and she was still spoiling him, but she couldn't help it. "All right, Tony, you can stay until I get out there this weekend. Then we're going to talk. Now put Mike on the phone, will you?"

Mike sounded excited. "Don't you think that's a neat idea, Mom? Uncle Tony said he'd pay me two dollars an hour."

"We'll talk about it this weekend. How's everything?"

"Fine. I think I'm going to get pretty good grades this year."

"Your grandpa okay?"

"Sure. Everything's okay out here, Mom. You don't have to worry about us."

She only wished that were true. She was beginning to think it was going to be easier to catch the strangler than to solve all the problems her family seemed to be having.

She wondered if Wynn ever had problems with his family, or if he even had a family. Probably they were nice, civilized people, the kind who never argued or shouted, a family whose men didn't have the kind of macho egos that the men in her family all had.

On the other hand, a nice quiet family might be boring. Still, she'd like the chance to find out.

Chapter Seven

"Wynn thinks you're the strangler."

Kyle, passing by her desk, did a double take. "Come again?"

Trying not to smile, Terry said, "He saw you watching me last night and got suspicious. Described you to me. I wouldn't be surprised if he reported you to the police."

"So he's got some smarts, huh, Rainkisser?" That had been his name for her ever since his first night in the closet. Unfortunately, the name seemed to be making the rounds of the precinct and she only hoped it would be forgotten in a few days. Until then, she ignored it.

"I don't know about you, Kyle, but I'm getting tired of working out every night."

"Maybe tonight'll be your lucky night," he said with a smirk.

"You mean maybe I'll get strangled?"

Kyle just laughed and walked away.

All the information they had come up with so far on Le Club's employees had turned out negative. With the exception of minor traffic violations and one arrest for possession, all the employees had come up clean—no police records and, as far as they knew, no backgrounds of mental instability.

That put them right back at the starting gate and they were all beginning to despair of catching the strangler before he killed again.

Terry got a phone call that morning from her sister-in-law, who said, "It's a good job, Terry, and we need the money. I'm making more than Tony made, plus I get full medical coverage for the family."

Being paid more than Tony was probably half her brother's problem. "I think you did the right thing, Joanna. I suppose you know Tony's staying on my boat."

"Yeah, Frank called me. Well, as far as I'm concerned, he can sulk over there as long as he likes."

"He wants to use my boat to take people out fishing."

"You gonna let him?"

"I don't know. What do you think?"

"That's up to you, Terry, but it doesn't sound like a bad idea. Tony always did love to fish."

Terry had been hoping to hear just the opposite so she'd have some justification for telling him no. She still didn't like the idea of her home being used as a floating bar for fishermen, which she knew would be what it would amount to.

It used to be that by Thursday she'd begin to look forward to the weekend, to just relaxing on the boat and being with Mike. Now, with Friday just a day away and no chance of seeing Wynn, except briefly at Le Club on Friday night, she found she no longer looked forward to weekends.

Pop, who used to be both friend and confidant to her, was seldom around anymore. Mike was at the age where he more and more preferred the company of his friends. Kathy would be sure to bend her ear all weekend regarding Johnny. And now her brother would be sleeping on the deck and was no doubt already summoning up a multitude of arguments over why she should allow him use of her boat.

She didn't feel ready for any of it.

WYNN WASN'T LOOKING FORWARD to the weekend, either. He liked the idea of going out to Fire Island after a hectic week in the city; it was the reality he didn't like. Everyone he knew in the city also spent weekends on the island, so except for the sea and the sand, the social life was much the same.

He was tired of hearing about people's relationships or lack of them, of hearing clothes discussed and seeing them shown off, of working on tans just so that the clothes would look better—of the whole Seventh Avenue social scene, to tell the truth.

What he wanted to do was to see Terry on the weekend. He didn't care if he had to go all the way to Brooklyn to do it. Ideally, he'd like to get her out to his house, but for some reason he didn't think he had a hope of that.

The little amount of time he had spent with her wasn't enough. He would have liked an entire day, maybe even a day and a night, to see once and for all if they were as compatible as he thought they might be, although all indications up to this point said that they weren't. But indications weren't everything. His deepest feelings told him that they could be very compatible.

And just maybe, if he really got to know her, he'd get over the obsession he was going through that caused him to sketch her when he should have been running his business, and to look for her face in every model who appeared at his showroom.

Heretofore never given to obsessions, he was beginning to worry.

At least, if he couldn't see her over the weekend, he didn't see any reason why their seeing each other had to be confined to the nights they worked out together. Take tonight, for instance. Where was it written that he couldn't see her on a Thursday?

Of course, she had never given him her phone number, and he didn't have the slightest idea whether she worked out of her apartment or an office. Picking up the phone book, he looked in it to find her number. There were several Caputos listed, but no Terry or even T. That figured. Most women in the city had unlisted numbers.

She also wasn't listed under interior decorators. Not ready to give up yet, he called the Society of Interior Decorators and inquired as to whether she was a member. The answer was negative, which didn't surprise him. Nothing about her appeared to be easy, so why should this be?

THURSDAY WAS A WASHOUT at Le Club. Not only were there very few women—blond, brunette or redhead—but the men seemed to be shying away from the women. Terry overheard a couple of the women discussing it, and they came to the conclusion that none of the men wanted to be mistaken for the strangler.

It made sense, but it didn't make her job easier.

She got home and was fixing herself a submarine sandwich when the buzzer sounded. She instantly froze, knowing no one was expected. If it was the strangler, she was in trouble. Kyle wasn't around, and while she should have prepared in advance for this eventuality, she had hardly given it a thought.

She got her gun out of her handbag and shoved it down between the cushions of the couch, then, as the buzzer sounded for a second time, she went to the door and looked through the peephole.

Seeing it was Wynn, she momentarily relaxed, then got tense again wondering why he was there.

She opened the door, leaving the chain on, and said, "What are you doing here?"

She could tell by the expression on his face that her question had struck him as rude, and on reflection it also struck her as rude. So she closed the door, undid the chain and opened the door wide.

"You aren't listed in the phone book," he said in explanation.

"I know. Come on in."

He was wearing white duck pants and a navy-blue blazer, despite the heat, and she thought he looked like an advertisement of the well-dressed New York man.

He stepped inside, saying, "You do have a phone, don't you?"

"Are *you* listed?" she asked, knowing very well he wasn't, because she had looked for his number on the first night she met him.

"It's surprising how big the phone book is," he said, "considering that I don't know anyone who's listed."

"I was just fixing a submarine. You want one?" she asked him. Now that he was there she hoped he'd stick around for a while. Having him there in person was a lot better than just thinking about him.

"I was going to ask you if you wanted to go out and eat."

Terry shook her head. "I just got home from Le Club. I feel like staying in."

"Why were you working out tonight?"

More lies, she thought, a sigh coming out unbidden. "I'm working out every night."

"What for?"

"I don't know," she said, improvising. "I guess I was so gung ho at first it sounded good. Now I'm not so sure."

She went back into the kitchen and he followed her. He watched for a minute as she piled several kinds of meat and cheese, then slices of tomato, onto the bread. He finally said, "I'll take one if you have enough."

"More than enough," she assured him, pointing him toward the refrigerator. "Why don't you get us each a beer?"

Sandwiches and cans of beer in hand, they walked through the open doors to the yard. Wynn took off his jacket and hung it neatly over the back of a chair before sitting down. This made her smile because she seldom gave any thought to her own clothes. And Mike was worse.

Wynn said, "I just didn't see why we could only see each other on workout nights."

"No reason at all," agreed Terry, talking with her mouth full, but not caring.

"In fact, I was going to try to persuade you to come out to Fire Island for part of the weekend. If you can tear yourself away from your boat, that is."

Terry thought about it. "That's a long way from Brooklyn."

"I'll come to Brooklyn, then."

That didn't take any thought at all. "No, I think I'd rather see Fire Island."

"You've never been there?"

"No, just heard about it."

"So does that mean you'll come out? We could go out together Friday night on the seaplane, and I'd send you back the same way Saturday if you want."

"You mean spend the night there?"

"I have a guest room; in fact, two." But his eyes were telling her she wasn't going to get anywhere near either if he could help it.

That arrangement was fine with her, as she wasn't sure she wanted to use one. She also knew that he wouldn't give her a hard time either way, which was reassuring.

"It sounds pretty good," she said, trying to hide her elation. And what made it really workable was that her brother could entertain Mike until she got to Brooklyn on Saturday.

"Does that mean you'll come?"

She smiled at him. "Yes, I'd like to."

"Great," he said, smiling back at her. "Since you worked out tonight, why don't we skip it tomorrow night and get an early start?"

"I can't do that," said Terry.

"Why not? I would think four nights a week would be enough."

"No, I really have to work out tomorrow night," she hedged, remembering at the same time that she wasn't supposed to be seeing him at all. But surely Friday night would be all right. Friday nights she was usually in Brooklyn anyway.

He looked baffled but didn't give her an argument. "Some friends of mine are having a party tomorrow night if you want to drop in on it. We wouldn't have to stay long."

"I don't mind," she said, then thought of another problem. "Can you drive to Fire Island?"

"No, but you can drive to Sayville and then get the ferry over. Why, you want me to rent a car?"

"I just thought it would be easier if I took mine. Then I wouldn't have to come back here for it."

"I didn't know you had one."

"Mill Basin is just about impossible to get to without one."

"Sure. Bring it to the club and we'll go from there."

They were both smiling now, their eyes locking until one of them would glance away, and then they'd lock again. Terry was feeling an excitement she hadn't felt in years, and to judge by the way Wynn was looking and acting, he was just as excited. That surprised her; she was sure he was used to inviting women out to his house. It was perfectly normal and she couldn't fault him for it. She was the one who'd been having the abnormal social life. In fact, no social life at all.

He didn't stay much longer after that, which was fine with Terry because she wanted to look through her clothes to see if she had anything that would do in a pinch for a party.

She didn't. It wasn't an insurmountable problem, though; she'd simply go shopping on her lunch hour the next day and find something. She didn't want to embarrass Wynn by showing up at a Fire Island party looking like an off-duty cop.

TONY HAD SOUNDED delighted on Friday when Terry asked him if he'd entertain his nephew that night. She wasn't dumb enough not to know the way his thought processes worked, that he was sure that by ingratiating himself in this way she'd see clear to let him use her boat. She didn't know how to refuse him, anyway. She found it hard to refuse her family anything, particularly this brother, who was two years younger than she and had followed her around as a child.

But he wasn't going to spend the summer sleeping on her deck; that was definitely out. Using the boat would be tied in to the stipulation that he go back home to Joanna. That might not be doing Joanna any big favor, but the boat was barely adequate for two. Besides, she hoped they'd get the killer before the summer was over, which meant she'd be there every night.

At the end of their conversation, Tony said, "Listen, Terry, I think there's something you ought to know."

"What now?" she asked, thinking the only relative left to surprise her was her grandmother. But what Granny could be up to, she couldn't imagine.

"It's Pop," said Tony. "He's moved his girlfriend in with him."

"I don't believe this."

"You met her yet?"

"I had the pleasure," said Terry, not bothering to hide her sarcasm.

"Cindi's not so bad."

So all the men were siding with sweet little Cindi, were they? "Well, I'll tell you, Toni—I'd think she was too young for you, let alone Pop."

"So Pop's going through his second childhood. I say, let him have his fun."

"Just tell me what's the point of giving Mike a good Catholic education when his grandfather is living in sin next door?"

"You'd prefer he married her?"

Naturally she didn't. "What's Mike got to say about it?"

"He's cool. He's no child, Terry. He knows what's going on whether she's living next door or Pop spends nights at her place. And they seem to get along well, together—Mike and Cindi, I mean."

"I'm sure they do—they both act the same age."

"As I said, give Pop time. And don't worry about Mike. We're going to a science fiction movie tonight."

At least Terry was spared from having to go, a small blessing in itself.

LE CLUB WAS EVEN DEADER than it had been on Thursday. The few people there seemed to keep to themselves, and even Scott wasn't as friendly as usual.

"This place is like a morgue tonight," she said to him, then realized how tasteless that must have sounded. "Sorry, I didn't mean that," she said, trying to reassure him.

But Scott seemed to find it amusing. "Yeah, everyone's running scared," he said. "I give you credit for guts—you're one of the few blondes to persevere."

"You notice I'm keeping my hair in a braid, though. Braided, it's not long enough to strangle me with."

Teasing, he reached out and grabbed her braid, then tried to wrap it around her neck. Giving up, he grinned at her. "You have guts—I like that."

"Thanks for the vote of confidence," she told him, checking out Kyle's whereabouts across the floor. Then she saw that Wynn—surreptitiously, to be sure—was also checking on Kyle. And Kyle, now aware of it, was starting to glower.

That face, she would swear, really did make him look like a killer. She had half a mind to go over and start flirting with Kyle just to see Wynn's reaction, but desisted in the cause of peace. Peace at work, that is.

She was waiting in the Jeep out in front when Wynn came out of the building. She called to him and saw his look of surprise when he saw the Jeep. But that was nothing new; he was always looking surprised, it seemed.

"I like it," he said, getting in and then having a hard time getting the door to stay shut. She reached across him and gave the door a good slam, then pulled off before Kyle could show up and see that she was disobeying orders again.

"I wouldn't have figured you for a Jeep," he said, a remark she was sure she had heard before. Only it had had something to do with her job last time.

"What would you figure me for?"

"Um, maybe a Chevy."

That meant no class, and she frowned at him. "Well, thanks a lot, Ransome. I'd figure you for a Caddy."

"And your reason?"

"They're pretentious."

He just laughed. "Any particular color?"

"Sure, several—to match your outfits."

"Well, at least your Jeep isn't pink and gray." That was a joke; the original paint could barely be detected.

He seemed amused at everything she said that night, but his amusement stopped when it started to rain and he found out that the Jeep didn't have a top.

"You mean you just get wet when it rains?" he asked, sounding incredulous.

"And snowed on when it snows."

"You don't mind?"

"I've gotten used to it."

He was shaking his head. "Every time I think I'm starting to figure you out, something happens that makes me have to start all over again. An interior decorator in a plush apartment driving a not-so-new Jeep. It doesn't scan."

She knew it didn't and was finding it as disconcerting as he was.

He, however, was more predictable. The house on Fire Island turned out to be every bit as classy as the way he dressed. Understated, to be sure, but pure class all the way. It was spacious, furnished with comfort in mind, and from the white tile floors to the blue denim slipcovers, it pleased her.

"I like it," she told him. "I couldn't have done a better job of decorating it myself." Actually, she couldn't have come near it.

"This was my own doing," he told her. "It's my place in town I got a decorator in for, and that's only because I didn't have the time to spend on it."

So he was artistic and she wasn't; she could live with that. She was probably better with a gun than he was.

He showed her into a guest room with an adjoining bath, and she got out of her wet clothes, rebraided her hair and got into the dress she had bought for the party. It had cost her more than she usually spent on clothes, but she wanted to look good for him.

Kathy had informed her that when in doubt, black always looked right, so she had bought a black silk dress with a ruffle over one shoulder and another one at the bottom of the short skirt. With it she was wearing black sandals with small heels. The bathroom had a full-length mirror on the back of the door, and she thought she looked pretty damn good. Black seemed to set off her blond hair better than the colors she usually wore.

When she returned to the living room, Wynn, in shorts and a T-shirt, said, "You look lovely. I'll be ready in a minute."

She was looking over his record collection—mostly classical, with a few Broadway albums—when he came back in gray slacks and a white shirt. "There'll be food at the party, but we could stop and eat on the way if you like," he said.

"I'm not that hungry," she told him, although she thought it was mostly nerves. It wasn't so much that she was meeting Wynn's friends for the first time, it was more that she would have to go on and on with her lies. And the next time they met her, if they ever did, she might have to rescind all those lies, and that wouldn't be a whole lot of fun.

They walked to the party along the beach, which wasn't easy in her sandals. The rain had stopped and the air was clear and fresh, and holding hands with Wynn on a beautiful beach wasn't the worst thing in the world.

She found out what the worst thing in the world was when they got to the party: Everyone there except her and Wynn was in shorts and T-shirts, and most of them were barefoot. That explained the fact that he had been in shorts when she came out of the guest room. And to make her feel less stupid, he had immediately changed. She appreciated the gesture, but wished he had just told her she was dressed all wrong.

If she had wanted to stand out at the party, she had picked the right way to do it. Every woman there was looking over her dress, and some of the men were asking Wynn if he had come straight from work.

She was introduced to so many people she didn't even try to keep their names straight, but during the course of the evening, she found that they all knew her name. Naturally they did. She was the freak who had shown up in a dress.

More than once she found herself wishing she were safely on her boat in Brooklyn. She was a fraud—a nice Brooklyn lady, a cop—trying unsuccessfully to impersonate one of the beautiful people, and failing miserably.

She felt she would have preferred to be strangled than have to go through with this.

Wynn, to his credit, got her out of the party early. As soon as they were back on the beach, he said, "I'm sorry, Terry. I should've warned you it would be casual."

"I guess I should've asked."

"I only say that because I could see it bothered you. But don't let it. If I liked you for the way you dressed, we wouldn't even be here."

"Thanks. I suppose."

"I apologize. That didn't come out sounding right. The fact is, I think you look lovely in that dress. Anyway, I think you're right and everyone else is wrong. You're the only one who dresses right to work out, and you were the only one dressed for a party tonight. If any of them didn't like it, the hell with them."

"I'll survive, Wynn."

"I know. It's just that I wanted you to have a great time out here."

"I'm not leaving yet," she reminded him.

He put his arm around her waist and squeezed her. "I'm aware of that."

Several replies came to mind; only the fact that they were heading for his house—alone—made her swallow them.

But they were heading there, and they were alone, plus they'd be alone together in the house all night. And that was something she had given a great deal of thought to—although not sufficient thought, because she still didn't know what she expected to come of it.

She was no longer a teenager with Nick, taught by the nuns to protect her virginity until her marriage. Even then, she had not held out once they were out of high school. Still, despite the fact that she was no kid and had not had a dearth of sexual experience in her marriage, she had no experience at all with casual sex.

That is, if it would be casual sex with Wynn. Although what else could it be when he might never speak to her again once he found out what an impostor she was?

She finally came to the conclusion that she would do whatever seemed comfortable. If she felt like sharing his room, she would; if she had any misgivings about it, she wouldn't.

But the decision was taken out of her hands the minute he stopped on the beach and pulled her close to him. The floodgates suddenly opened wide, and all the feelings she had held back since her husband's death started to bombard her senses. The way he was kissing her was nothing like the way he had kissed her good-night. That had been lovely, but this was damn near overwhelming. She didn't demur for a second when he led her into the house and straight to his bedroom. She didn't even notice the decor—in fact, that was the furthest thing from her mind.

Their clothes were off without her even being aware of how it happened, and then they were on the bed. Then it was darkness and heat, the gradual melting of the self, the sound of quickening breath and beating hearts, of hands sliding on sweating skin. His mouth over hers, their breaths mingling, he was molding her with his hands, turning her flesh to clay, stroking and squeezing her into something she had not been before: a passive creature, acquiescent, spreading herself in complete surrender.

She felt herself opening out to receive him. Something hot and hard touched her, withdrew, returned again, and her body rising and falling, became a pool of sensation. Then it slid into her, dividing her and warming her, making her melt and pour all around it while it moved in her hidden depths. Everything that she had been, all her separate parts, became one extraordinary, pulsating well of pleasure, raising her up through various levels of passion to pure, limitless feeling.

She moved against him and with him, trying to hold on to her senses, losing them and getting them back again and finally losing them totally.

At last they lay together in the near darkness, one on top of the other, letting the night surround them with the song of its silence, until he pulled his head back and seemed to be studying her.

"You never cease to surprise me," he said, but he said it in a tone of awe.

He rolled off her and lay beside her, clasping her fingers in his hand, his face turned to hers as he seemed to wait for her to say something.

She tried to return his gaze calmly, but she could still feel him inside of her, every nerve recording his presence. She was glowing inside and felt the same glow radiating from him.

"That was...unexpected," she said.

"Yes. Unexpected and perfect."

She thought maybe she should break the mood, interject some nonsense that would make him laugh.

Instead, she rolled toward him, one hand nestling beneath his chin. She knew she was in love, and it wasn't a joking matter.

SHE FELT SHY with him in the morning. No words of love had been spoken by either of them, but the air was filled with the tension of unspoken feelings.

He fixed her breakfast and they ate silently, exchanging smiles often. She wished she could stretch the moments out until they became a single strand between them.

When they had finished eating, he said, "You want to get some sunbathing in before you go?"

"Yes," she said, wanting to lie beside him on the sand and feel his closeness. The night before didn't seem quite real in the daylight, but the way her body was feeling was real. Real and long overdue.

She was just coming out of the bathroom in her swimsuit when the phone rang. He answered it, then handed it to her.

She covered the mouthpiece of the phone and said, "I had to leave my number with my father," not thinking how juvenile that must sound.

Then, "Hi, Pop," she said. "What's up?"

"Everything's fine here, but your lieutenant wants you to call. I said I'd pass on the message."

"I'll call him right away," she said, but Pop interrupted with, "And I won't ask why a man answered the phone, Terry."

"Good, 'cause it's none of your business," she told him, thinking she could be as mysterious as he.

She looked over at Wynn, and with some sixth sense of his he said, "I'll be out on the beach." Then he left her alone to make her call.

The lieutenant's first words were, "You better get in here fast. He killed again last night, Terry, and this time I think we've got a witness."

"Oh, my God," she said, brought back to the real world with a jolt. "I'll be there as soon as I can, but I'm on Fire Island."

"What the hell... You're with Wynn Ransome, aren't you?"

"I'm sorry, Lieutenant, but since it's the weekend—"

"We'll discuss that later. Take the plane in; it'll be faster."

She was dressed before she realized what this latest murder meant. It couldn't have been Wynn, he had been with her, which meant there wasn't any reason why she couldn't tell him now. She could finally confess that she'd been lying to him the whole time.

The prospect gave her pause as she packed her bag. She'd confess, but not now. Not in a hurry, when all she had to say to him would take time. And maybe, too, she was a little afraid of his reaction. And yet, if last night was any indication, she thought it would be all right.

She ran out to the beach, carrying her bag, and flung herself down in the sand beside him. "You're not the strangler," she cried, leaning down to give him a kiss.

"What're you yelling about?"

"I've got to go. It's an emergency and I don't have time to explain now. Will you show me where I can get the seaplane?"

"What about your Jeep?"

"Could you drive it into the city for me, Wynn? Listen, if you bring it in Sunday night, I'll meet you. There's something I've got to tell you."

"Every time I think I've solved the mystery, it's something else," he said, but he was already getting up.

"I'd tell you now, but it would take some time and I've got to get back to the city fast."

"I won't even ask any questions," he said, grabbing her hand and holding it tight.

She tried to keep all thoughts of another dead woman out of her mind until she was away from him. She'd been able to compartmentalize her life before—home separate, work separate—and until they reached the seaport she held tight to the thought of her and Wynn together.

Right before she boarded the plane, he said, "Just one thing, Terry," and she hoped he wasn't going to ask her about the remark she had made about his not being the strangler. It had popped out without her thinking about it.

"Are you listening to me?" he asked her.

"I'm listening, Wynn."

"I'm really not sure how you view me or my lifestyle, but last night—"

"You don't have to say anything, Wynn."

"I just want to tell you, I took it very seriously."

"So did I."

"Good. Then I'll see you Sunday night."

It wasn't until later that she wondered how seriously he would take it when he heard the truth.

Chapter Eight

"He's changed his MO," said Kyle, looking down at the body, half on, half off, the living room couch.

"Probably out of desperation," said Terry. "There aren't many blondes left at Le Club—most of them panicked, I think." She took another look at the body. The woman had the kind of muscles Terry would like to develop.

"Maybe," said Kyle, "and maybe not. It could be someone copying the MO, someone who wanted her killed and have it blamed on the strangler."

"Maybe, but I have a feeling it's the same person," said Terry.

The lieutenant was also there, looking sporty in Bermuda shorts and a tank top. "For the time being we'll treat it as one of the strangler's, unless the autopsy comes up with any significant differences."

"Who's the witness?" Terry asked.

Kyle said, "The woman in the other apartment on this floor. She was behind him on the stairs when he came up. She saw him stop outside the victim's door."

"Was she suspicious?" asked Terry.

"What for? Would you have been?"

"Why don't you talk to her, Terry," said the lieutenant. "Women often open up more to other women." Plus, Kyle was often abrasive with witnesses, a fact of which Terry knew the lieutenant was aware.

Molly Fogarty, an attractive woman in her late fifties, opened the door to Terry. When Terry showed her police ID, she was immediately invited in. The apartment had the same floor plan as that of the victim, but there the resemblance ended. The victim's apartment had been cluttered; this one was starkly furnished and had the same air of elegance about it as Molly Fogarty had.

"I understand you might be able to identify the murderer," said Terry, taking the proffered chair.

"I can't swear he's the murderer," said Fogarty, "but I saw a man going to Sheila's apartment last night about ten."

"Would you be able to identify him if you saw him again?"

"Maybe. From the back. I never did see his face."

Too bad, thought Terry. On the other hand, if the woman had gotten a look at his face, she might have been killed, too. "What can you tell me about him?"

"Muscular. Rather like the other policeman I talked to."

Another person fingering Kyle. "Could you get any idea of his height or weight?"

"I'd say he was a good six feet. I'm not good at judging weight, but he was very well built without being fat. His muscles fairly rippled as he walked up those stairs."

"What about hair color?"

"He had his head down, and the stairs aren't all that well lit, but I got the impression he had blond hair. But I think he might have been wearing a baseball cap that could have been light-colored. You understand, officer, that I wasn't paying that much attention. Most of the time my eyes were on the stairs."

Too bad she wasn't certain; if the man did have blond hair that would eliminate a lot of the suspects. "Do you recall what he was wearing?"

"Nikes. The name of the shoes was written on the back. Jeans, but not blue. I'd say they were khaki. And a striped T-shirt, maybe navy and white. But it could have been black and white."

"That's good," said Terry. "Was there anything else about him you can remember?"

"Just that he wasn't panting. These stairs kill me, but he wasn't the least out of breath. And he was carrying a brown paper bag in one hand. A small one—lunch bag size."

Terry thanked her for her help, then went back and talked to Kyle and the lieutenant.

"Not much," agreed Kyle, "but more than we've had up to now."

They were just deciding to go back to the precinct house when one of the uniformed officers came in and said, "Her boyfriend's outside, Lieutenant."

They exchanged glances. Then the lieutenant said, "Hold him outside, Bill. We'll be right out."

"A boyfriend," whispered Terry. "Do you think..."

"Not likely," said Kyle. "If he offed her, he wouldn't show up the next day."

"Unless he was very smart," said Lieutenant Corbet.

Terry couldn't help thinking that she hoped it was the boyfriend. That way they wouldn't have to break the bad news to him.

They went outside and Terry stopped dead in her tracks. The man facing her looked just as surprised. He seemed to recover first and said, "What are you doing here?"

Lieutenant Corbet gave her a questioning look, and she said, "I met him at Le Club, Lieutenant. He was helping me out with the weights one night."

"What is this? What's happening?" the man asked, but Terry could tell by his eyes that he suspected the worst. Or maybe he already knew and was acting.

With a nod from the lieutenant, Terry said, "We're police officers. I understand you were asking about Sheila."

The man's tan seemed to fade. "Is this the strangler thing?"

He appeared genuinely shaken, and Terry instinctively reached out to put a hand on his arm. "I'm sorry," she said. Then she looked down and saw that he was wearing Nikes. She was about to say something, but the lieutenant had taken over and was asking for some ID, then reading him his rights. And by then Terry had noticed that both Kyle and the lieutenant were also wearing Nikes, as, no doubt, were half the people in the city on any given day.

"Jesus, you think I did it?" the man, now identified as Jeff Sanger, kept saying over and over. Terry felt a rush of sympathy when his eyes filled with tears, which spilled out to run down his face unheeded. Could he be that good an actor?

She remembered his telling her that his girlfriend was a serious bodybuilder, and how he had been helpful to her but hadn't come on to her at all. A part of her wanted him to be the strangler. She wanted the case to be over, no more women to be killed.

But she didn't believe it.

The next thing Terry knew, Kyle was leading Sanger out of the building, and she followed along with the lieutenant. Sanger wasn't in cuffs—he hadn't been arrested—but she knew that was only a matter of time unless he had a damn good alibi for the time of the victim's death.

She rode in the car with Lieutenant Corbet, and as soon as she had fastened her seat belt he asked her, "What do you think?"

"I felt sorry for him. Did you see the tears in his eyes?"

"I've seen killers break down and cry before. So have you."

"Sure, but not before they've confessed."

"Maybe that's why he returned. He probably wanted to get caught."

"It doesn't make sense," said Terry. "If she was his girlfriend, why would he be killing other women?"

"Why not? Who says he has to make sense? You think strangling women makes sense?"

"It must make sense to the killer."

"Okay, Terry, let's suppose this: The guy's killing other women, for some reason unknown to us at the moment, and this Sheila finds out about it. He'd have to kill her, wouldn't he? To protect himself? And then maybe he felt remorse afterward and came back."

"He seemed so nice."

"Sure he did. If he didn't, he never would've gotten into those other women's apartments. And incidentally, Terry, what were you doing on Fire Island?"

"I'm sorry. I just figured since I was off duty..."

"You serious about this guy?"

Terry thought back to the night before. "I'm afraid so."

"Well, if he was with you last night, I guess that lets him off the hook. I take it he was with you."

"All night," she said, afraid to look over and see his reaction.

"Is he as classy as his clothes?"

"More," she said, and heard the lieutenant chuckle. "Does that mean I can level with him?"

"Yeah, go ahead. He has no reason not to keep his mouth shut. And maybe that way you'll stop undermining the operation, if there still is an operation."

When they got to the station and began questioning Sanger, he claimed to have been home alone the night before studying for his CPA exam, which had been held that morning.

"You took the exam?" asked Terry, and when he said yes, she wondered if a man who had just killed could sit through an exam.

"That's what I was doing at Sheila's," said Sanger, without being asked. "I was picking her up so we could celebrate."

They went over the dates of the other murders with him, but he seemed confused, too distraught to remember where he had been, let alone come up with an alibi.

"If I could see my appointment calendar," he said at one point, "I might be able to remember. Right now those dates are a blank."

Three hours later they let him go. His appointment calendar had been picked up from his office, and they had verified that one of the nights in question he and Sheila had been at his boss's house in Westchester for the weekend. Lots of witnesses.

Before he left, he turned to the lieutenant and said, "I think Le Club ought to be closed down."

"Then we might never catch him," said Lieutenant Corbet.

Looking ten years older than when she'd met him, Sanger said, "If you'd closed it down before, Sheila would still be alive."

After he left, Terry said, "We've got to think of some other way, Lieutenant. Obviously I'm not working out as a decoy—this time he preferred a brunette to me."

"You have any suggestions?" asked Lieutenant Corbet.

"Maybe you should get some more policewomen in there as decoys. Just numerically speaking, the chances of his picking me aren't good. There'd be a better chance if he had more choices."

"I'll see what I can do," said Lieutenant Corbet, but he didn't look hopeful.

An hour later no one had come up with any better ideas, and Terry finally left to go home, which meant taking a subway to the far reaches of Brooklyn, then a taxi to the marina.

She hadn't remembered to call home and was afraid they might be worried about her, but when she got to the boat no one was there. A look out the window told her Pop wasn't around, either.

There was evidence of people having been there, though, and she saw her brother's sloppy hand in the dirty dishes piled in the sink, the futon unrolled on the deck, the two saucers filled with cigarette butts and the trash filled with empty beer cans.

All of which she was going to put a stop to as soon as Tony showed up.

She couldn't help making the comparison between her small, sloppy boat and Wynn's beach house, and her mind instantly turned to thoughts of Wynn. She had a big problem. Now that she could finally be honest with him, she wasn't looking forward to the actual confession.

Last night had been perfect. But last night he thought he was making love to an interior decorator, a woman unencumbered with a child. She had thought at first of what a relief it would be not having to lie to him anymore, but what if he didn't like the truth when he heard it?

A female cop just might not be his idea of the ideal woman. In fact, it probably wouldn't even be a contender. For that matter, a lot of people didn't even like cops. Just take that party they had gone to. They might have thought she was dressed strangely but no one thought it strange that she did decorating for a living. But what would have happened if he had introduced her as one of New York's finest? Well, for one thing, statistically speaking, in any crowd that size with the kind of money those people made, some of them were no doubt carrying drugs. They wouldn't have been thrilled to have the law in their midst. For another, and she had noticed this before, a lot of people either clammed up or automatically acted guilty around cops. Not her family, but just about everyone else she met.

But even if Wynn turned out to be delighted that she was a cop—which was highly improbable—there was still the little matter of Mike. Maybe he didn't like kids. Or maybe he thought little kids were cute but drew the line at big-mouthed twelve-year-olds, for which she wouldn't blame him.

The effect the rest of her family might have on him was something she didn't even want to contemplate.

But say he liked cops. Say he even liked kids. Would he really think it was worth it to date someone who lived miles from the city and who couldn't, once this case was over, stay out all night? Sure, she got away with it last night, but she had done it with lies, this time to her brother. She had said it was work that was keeping her in the city, and they wouldn't question that, but unless she was working on some special case, that rarely happened. And furthermore, she didn't like the idea of having to lie about her whereabouts again.

And yet, despite all the difficulties she could foresee, Wynn was too good to just give up on. She hadn't thought she'd ever fall in love again. That love now seemed like a gift to her, and she wanted to hold it to her and treasure it.

It was late afternoon by the time she had finished cleaning. The temperature was in the nineties, probably higher in the boat, and she went up on deck to get some air. It was even hotter in the sun, and she was thinking of driving over to see Kathy, who had an air-conditioned apartment, when she remembered that her means of transportation was still out on Fire Island.

Feeling hot, sweaty, rejected by her family and a virtual prisoner without her Jeep, she was about to go back down to the cabin and take another cold shower when she saw Mike coming down the dock.

"Where's your uncle Tony?" she asked him when he jumped on board.

He shrugged.

"Weren't you with him?"

"I was playing baseball with the guys."

Well, maybe he'd gone home. She hoped he'd gone home.

"Where's your grandpa?"

He shrugged again. "Went somewhere with Cindi, I think."

"So what're you doing tonight? Want to go to a movie?" She felt guilty enough to sit through even another science fiction epic.

"There's a street fair at St. Cecilia's. Some of the guys are going."

"Some of the guys" meant she wasn't welcome. "Want to go see Great-grandma Caputo tomorrow?" Mike's paternal grandparents had retired to Arizona, but she liked to take him to see Nick's grandmother at least once a month, not wanting Nick's family to feel left out.

She could see by his face that he wasn't thrilled, so she added, "We could go to Coney Island afterward."

"I guess so." That was better than no response at all. Then he said, "Where's the Jeep? I didn't see it."

She had again forgotten about that, but maybe Pop would let her use his car tomorrow. "I left it in the city."

Luckily, that didn't arouse his curiosity; she hadn't even thought up a good reason for leaving it there. She realized that for some reason she preferred lying to Wynn than to Mike, but maybe it was because her job dictated that she lie to Wynn. A guilty conscience was her reason for lying to Mike.

Terry concluded that she wouldn't be able to pick up the Jeep from Wynn on Sunday. She'd seen little enough of Mike this week; she couldn't cut the weekend any shorter just for her own pleasure. And, of course, that also effectively prolonged the time before she had to confess to Wynn.

"Aunt Kathy's called you about five times, Mom. I told her you'd call her."

"I will in a little while."

"And Aunt Rosa called."

"Okay." At least that gave her something to do that night—she could answer phone calls.

WYNN SPENT SATURDAY NIGHT home alone. There were always parties to go to on the island, and any bar would be filled with people he knew. Something had happened to him, though, that he wanted to examine, and for that he required quiet.

He did eat an early dinner out—lobster, a salad, a bottle of white wine. But afterward he headed home, electing to sit on his front porch and enjoy the fresh breeze coming in off the water.

Somewhere between yesterday and today, he had gone from being attracted to Terry without knowing why, to being in love with her and still not knowing why. And since he liked to know the whys and wherefores of everything he did, he felt it was something he'd better look into.

He wasn't fooling himself that the sex hadn't had a great deal to do with it. But sex had never made him fall in love before, and he didn't want to think that was all of it, because if it was all of it, he was a lot shallower than he had thought.

He didn't believe it possible that sex could be that good without deep feelings. Oh, it could be good, sometimes even great, but it was never earthshaking, and he'd be damned if it hadn't been earthshaking with Terry.

It had come as a big surprise to him, and he felt it had been equally surprising to her. They were two people who had barely even touched, but the first time they really did touch, they had both seemed to go out of control. No, not out of control, really—more just carried away. And at the end of it, he had felt he loved her. And instead of that feeling dissipating during the day, as he had half expected it to do, the feeling only increased, and it no longer had anything to do with the sex.

He could only remember being in love twice. The first time was in high school, and it had been as starry-eyed and romantic as first love always is. He couldn't even remember much about her now other than the fact that she had kept him in a constant state of lust, never satisfied by their gropings in the back seat of his car. Susan, that was her name. Susan Carruthers. And her father had been a doctor. He remembered that because she had supplied her girlfriends with birth control pills, something she had made a point of telling him.

Not that it had changed things. She still protected her virginity every time she was with him. He had never made a fuss about it, because he had felt lucky to be dating her. She had been pretty and popular and could have dated any one of the football players but instead had preferred him. He had never gone out for sports other than swimming. He thought it might be because his father hadn't liked sports, hadn't really had time for them, because he'd had to work even while in high school. Then, afterward, when he was building up his business, manufacturing clothes was his only interest.

In the affluent Long Island town his family had moved to when he was nine, sports weren't of primary importance anyway. Making good grades and being accepted into good colleges were the top priorities for the kids. He had wanted to go to Wharton, which had a fine business school. He had some nebulous notion of working on Wall Street, but in what capacity he wasn't sure. He had just known that he wanted to be one of the commuters to the city in a Brooks Brothers suit, briefcase in hand, going off every day to where the important things happened. If someone had told him then that he would end up designing clothes, he would have laughed. When it turned out later that he had a talent for designing, he had been the most surprised of anyone.

The second time he fell in love he had been in college, and this time he had fallen in love with one of his instructors. Her name was Margo, and she was in her thirties at the time. Late thirties he had thought then; in retrospect, he didn't think she had been that old.

On his part, it had merely been a great respect of her as a teacher at first. Unlike most romances between teacher and student, she had been the one to finally instigate things. It had lasted two years, and at the end of it he was left feeling he would never again meet her equal. He had loved her mind even more than her body, and except for an occasional reference to it by her, he never even thought of the difference in their ages.

In a way, he had been right; he never did meet her equal. Certainly none of the models he had gone with later had even begun to captivate his fancy the way Margo had.

For that matter, he wasn't sure Terry had. She was the most interesting woman he had met in years, but he wasn't sure that it had anything at all to do with her mind. It seemed to have more to do with the air of mystery about her. But at least she wasn't a model. She didn't glance into every available surface to reassure herself constantly about her looks; she didn't starve herself, was not anorexic; she didn't spend half her time shopping for clothes and the other half getting her beauty sleep. But then, there were probably lots of normal women in the world who didn't do all those things.

And maybe he was being too hard on models.

When Wynn was in his junior year of college, his father had had his heart attack, which meant that Wynn was forced to drop out, leave Margo and learn a business he had never had much interest in. It had, he admitted, gone to his head when all those gorgeous models suddenly began falling all over him. He hadn't kidded himself; it happened because he was suddenly head of a fashion house, which meant work if he dated them, and the good life if he should marry one of them.

If Terry had set out to captivate him, it couldn't have worked better. First there was her presence at the party, which only pointed up to him how shallow all the other women at the party were. Then there was her abandonment in bed, which resulted in the most memorable sexual experience he had ever had—not that Margo hadn't been something else in bed, but he hadn't been experienced enough at the time to appreciate it. Then, when he wouldn't have believed she could top that, there was her sudden appearance on the beach this morning, her saying some strange words to the effect that he wasn't the strangler, then her escape to the city saying that they had to talk, leaving him, of course, thinking of nothing else for the rest of the day.

He wasn't the strangler? He hadn't for a moment ever thought she'd seriously thought he was. Had she harbored some doubts, then been assured when she woke up that morning still alive? Not that he'd blame her for having doubts. If, at this time, he were a female member of Le Club, he was sure he'd have doubts about every man he came into contact with there. But if she really had doubts, would she have gone to Fire Island with him in the first place?

Well, she wasn't the only one who wanted to talk. Twice models had moved in with him briefly; both times it had been a disaster. He had about given up on the idea that he'd ever spend his life with a woman, but Terry had already changed his mind about that. He had always wanted a normal life. His parents' marriage had been happy. His mother, now a widow, was growing older and thinner in her condo in Fort Lauderdale, and there wasn't a time he had talked to her on the phone when she hadn't brought his father into the conversation. If he had gone into any other profession, by now he probably would have met a woman with whom he could settle down. No one had forced him to date models. It was just that he was constantly in contact with them—and he wasn't immune to their looks—so it just seemed to transpire.

He felt he'd like to live with Terry. He liked having her around. In fact, without her today he felt incomplete. He wasn't that crazy about her apartment, except for the garden, of course, but if she didn't want to live in his larger place, he'd willingly sublet it to move in with her. Or better yet, maybe they should get a different place altogether, one with no memories for either of them.

That made him realize how little he really knew about her. Not that he had told her much about his background, either. Certainly they'd never gotten around to discussing former lovers, but as far as he was concerned, that was to the good. Every time a woman started telling him about previous affairs, he could project into the future, when she'd be discussing him in the same way. So, no, he didn't regret that they hadn't yet had that particular conversation.

He wondered if she liked old movies. Thirties movies. He collected them, and some nights, when he needed to unwind, he would go to bed early, put one in his VCR and lose himself in another time. He wasn't quite sure why those movies pleased him more than the movies that were currently out. Maybe it was the clothes. The elegance. The women were beautiful and tough, and the men were handsome and charming. There was a romanticism to them that was lacking in current films.

He didn't even know her age. He really only knew three facts about her, and couldn't swear to any of them. She said she was an interior decorator; she said she had a boat in Brooklyn, unlikely though that might sound; and she appeared to be a good cook, although for all he knew, she might have bought that spaghetti dinner prepared. Certainly it took no culinary skills to make a submarine sandwich.

And it would seem she had a father, judging by what he overheard her say on the telephone this morning. All of this added up to less than he knew about any of his employees.

None of it really fit. She didn't seem like an interior decorator. She didn't seem the type to be working out at Le Club. She didn't even seem to be a real blonde. Just maybe she could be someone with a boat in Brooklyn. He didn't know about that because he'd never known anyone with a boat in Brooklyn.

The father he'd concede her; he had no problem with that. Although he couldn't figure out why a grown woman would leave a phone number where she could be reached by her father. He wasn't even going to try to figure that out.

That gave him the first constructive idea he had had all evening. He went inside, called information for Brooklyn, and to his great surprise, found that a T. Caputo was indeed listed. But other than making a note of the number, he didn't do anything about it. She had never told him not to call her in Brooklyn; more importantly, she had never told him he could.

He thought of getting up early in the morning and returning her Jeep to her in Brooklyn. It only took him about two seconds to think better of it. It would in a sense be checking up on her, taking her unaware, unprepared. For that matter, he didn't even know how to get to Brooklyn.

She had said she'd be back in the city on Sunday. He'd deliver her Jeep to her apartment and leave a note in it asking her to call him. Strange, they had never even talked on the phone. He didn't think he'd ever made love to a woman without having first talked to her on the phone.

But then in a lot of ways Terry was turning out to be a first.

But why had she run off like that this morning? The hell with it. It was just one more mystery that he hoped would be cleared up tomorrow.

KATHY DECIDED to join them on their outing to Coney Island. Jenny, Kathy's teenager, didn't go along, but the two younger kids did, annoying Mike no end because he was expected to look out for them.

Great-grandmother Caputo had also gone along, and Terry was glad she had invited her when she saw how much the woman was enjoying the afternoon on the beach. Wearing a flowered housedress, and sitting up knitting beneath an umbrella, she appeared to be having a good time just being around other people. Terry vowed to include her more often in family activities; with her own family scattered around the country, she must be lonely.

While the children played in the water, Terry and Kathy rubbed suntan lotion all over themselves and spread out on towels beside Great-grandma Caputo. It was a hot Sunday and the beach was crowded with families. Radios were turned to either the Mets game or rock music, the young vying with the old. Terry reached over and turned Mike's radio off, but the same station was being played by several nearby radios and she might as well not have bothered.

Looking down at herself, Terry could already see in her body the results of her working out. The muscles in her arms were pronounced when she flexed them and her thighs were much firmer. Her stomach, which hadn't been a problem to begin with, hadn't flattened out any, but her stomach muscles were getting strong. She glanced at Kathy. Although Kathy was only two years older, her body was already beginning to spread. But then, Kathy had had three kids and Terry had only one. Having children could be disastrous to a body.

Kathy's ample hips revealed the family trait that so far Terry had managed to avoid but one that she expected any day to start showing up on her. It was all very well for the relatives to say she had her father's hips, but she knew that Italian women were never built like Italian men.

Kathy was being unnaturally quiet, and Terry was beginning to doze off, thinking that the presence of Great-grandma Caputo was no doubt serving to make her sister keep her problems to herself. But she had no sooner thought that than Kathy said, "I don't know what to tell the kids. They keep asking me where Johnny is."

"They're too old to lie to," said Terry, noticing at the same time how Great-grandma Caputo's ears began to perk up.

Kathy, as though sensing this, looked at the old woman and said, "My husband left me for another woman."

Great-grandma Caputo, who had no doubt heard worse in her time, merely nodded.

"What do you think I ought to do, Terry?" asked Kathy.

Once again she was supposed to know everything. "What do you feel like doing?"

"You really want to know? I feel like putting the kids in the car and delivering them to that woman's house. See how well they get along with three kids around all the time."

Terry saw Great-grandma Caputo smiling at that. "That might solve the problem of Johnny and the other woman," said Terry, "but it wouldn't solve the problem of you and Johnny."

"What problem?" Kathy demanded. "We didn't have any problems until she came along."

Terry propped herself up on one elbow and looked at her sister. "I don't think that's true, Kath. I think what Johnny needs is some peace and quiet when he gets home, not the constant aggravation you give him."

Kathy sat bolt upright and looked ready to flee the beach. "What do you know about it?"

"I know what Johnny told me, and I also know how you are."

"He wants peace and quiet? You don't think I'd like a little of that? Let him have the kids all the time and see how much peace and quiet he gets."

"Then maybe you ought to think about getting out of the house."

Kathy gave her a scornful look. "You think a woman working solves everything."

"That's not true. I was happy staying at home. I just don't think you are. And it doesn't have to be work. You could go back to school."

"I'm thirty-five. I'm too old to go back to school."

"And you're too young to spend your days watching soap operas."

"She's right," said Great-grandma Caputo. "When you get to be my age you can watch the soaps. All the old people watch them."

"Did you ever work?" Kathy asked her.

The old woman shook her head slowly. "No, never. I didn't even finish high school."

"Well, that's all I finished," said Kathy, "and I don't know how to do anything. Anything that would make me money, anyway."

Terry could tell Kathy wasn't in any mood to accept advice, so she changed the subject. "I've been seeing a man," she said to Great-grandma Caputo, not wanting her to hear it first from Kathy, who, she knew, was bound to reveal the news sometime during the afternoon.

The old woman smiled at Terry in delight. "That's good, Terry. You've been alone too long. It's not good for a woman to be without a man."

Terry didn't think that was the greatest thing to say since Kathy was currently without one. But then, suddenly Great-grandma Caputo was asking, "Is he Catholic?" and Terry wished she hadn't brought the subject up.

"I don't know," she had to admit.

"I doubt it," said Kathy. "Wynn Ransome sounds pretty WASP to me."

Terry hadn't even thought of that. Still, it wasn't like in Great-grandma Caputo's day, when mixed marriages caused shock waves through families. And that was assuming he'd even want to marry her.

Then Kathy's youngest came up to sit with them and any serious talk came to a halt.

By six o'clock they were all agreeably tired and they had supper on the boardwalk before Kathy drove them all home.

Tony was on Pop's boat and called to Terry as she passed. "Can we talk some business?"

"Let me change first, Tony," she told him, wanting to take a shower and wash off the sand. She was hoping Tony would come over to her boat so she wouldn't have to see Cindi again, but he didn't.

Pop gave her a hug and Cindi smiled at her, and Terry tried to be friendly to both of them, but it took an effort. If anything, Cindi looked even younger today in some little outfit that looked like a child's rompers. And Pop, she noticed, was growing a mustache.

"Have you thought it over?" Tony asked.

"I've thought about it," she admitted. "But you can't live on my boat, Tony."

"Hey, no sweat. I'm back home now. Even Joanna thinks it's a good idea."

"And you're not going to object to her working?"

With a forced cheeriness, he said, "Anything that makes her happy." That was a turnabout, and if taking out charter fishermen was the cause of it, Terry was all for it.

"No weekends," Terry stipulated.

"No problem," said Tony. "Later, if it goes well, I'll get my own boat. And listen, Terry, I'll give you a percentage of the profits seeing as it's your boat."

"It's not mine," said Terry. "It's Pop's. All I ask is that it's clean when I get home."

"Can I work for him, Mom?" begged Mike.

"Sure. It'll keep you out of trouble."

Mike was grinning at his uncle and Tony was trying not to look too triumphant, but not succeeding. Then Cindi said, "We'd like you people to stay to dinner," and Terry instantly took offense. The young woman was now sounding like the mistress of the house. Or the boat. She was glad to be able to say they'd already eaten, even when she saw Pop's look of disappointment.

Well, if Pop thought he could ram his child lover down their throats, he was mistaken. She, for one, was not succumbing to Cindi's charms, even though the males in the family might be.

That night, though, when she was watching some inane TV program with Mike, she thought about how Pop had looked, and she had to admit that he seemed happy. She had never thought of him as being unhappy up until then, but Cindi seemed to be making a difference.

Was it jealousy? Had she had Pop to herself for so long that she resented Cindi's moving in with him? She didn't really think so. She thought it was more that she had always thought he had dignity. He hadn't been one of those men who ran around with a girl young enough to be his daughter. And now that he was, he seemed to have lost some of that dignity.

Hell, Cindi was the kind of girl Pop would have called a bimbo a few months ago. Well, now that bimbo had moved in with her father and maybe things were never going to be the same again.

"What do you think of Cindi?" she asked Mike during the next commercial break.

"She's okay."

"Do you see much of her?"

"I've been eating over there."

"Well, do you like her?"

He was looking a little guilty when he said, "Yeah, she's funny. If you'd get to know her, Mom, you'd see."

"Funny? You mean she tells jokes?" Probably the silly kind a kid would like.

"No, not jokes. She just says funny things. I don't know how to explain it."

Terry couldn't find one thing amusing about her father's young friend, but she didn't say so. Anyway, her son was certainly entitled to his own opinion without her trying to prejudice his views.

She was about to mention Wynn then, prepare Mike for him, but something stopped her. She might as well wait until after she told Wynn the truth. It could be that after that there'd be nothing to tell Mike anyway.

The whole thing was making her nervous.

Chapter Nine

When Terry hadn't called him by Sunday night, Wynn began to be worried. He had seen in the papers where another woman had been strangled, making him remember the brutish-looking man who had been watching Terry in the lobby of Le Club.

At midnight, unable to relax enough to go to bed, he took a taxi across town to Terry's apartment and rang the bell. There was no answer, and when he walked over to the curb where he had parked her Jeep, he saw that his note still lay on the seat.

Rationally, he knew she was no doubt still on her boat, had decided not to return to the city until the morning. Feeling a little foolish at how worried he was, he returned home, but sleep didn't come easily that night.

On Monday, just to assuage his fears, he again took a taxi over to her apartment before going to work. She still wasn't home and the note was still in the Jeep. Thinking that interior decorators could probably keep any hours they liked and that he was worrying unnecessarily, he went to work.

Le Club

At noon, though, instead of getting lunch, he went by her place again. And this time, seeing that she still hadn't returned, he decided to do something about it. Maybe she wouldn't appreciate it if she were all right, but if she weren't, if something had happened to her, he'd never forgive himself for not acting.

He made a phone call to the manager of Le Club, asking who was in charge of the case, and was given the name of a Lieutenant Corbet and the address of the precinct house.

When he got there, he was directed upstairs to the lieutenant's office. The lieutenant stood when he entered and held out his hand, and Wynn, despite his worry, didn't fail to notice that the lieutenant was dressed better than he was. In fact, the man could make a good living modeling if he ever decided to give up police work.

"Nice to meet you, Mr. Ransome," said the lieutenant. "Have a seat and let me hear what's bothering you."

"It's about the strangler."

"Yes, I assumed that."

Wynn leaned forward in the chair. "It could be nothing, of course, but I'm rather worried. There's a woman I've been seeing, a member of Le Club, and I'm concerned about her whereabouts. She was supposed to be back in the city last night but hasn't called me. I've warned her to be careful, and there was also this man one night who seemed to be watching her. I know it doesn't sound like much," he said, spreading out his arms, and then leaning back in the chair. He thought he caught a look of amusement in the lieutenant's eyes, which no doubt meant he wasn't going to be taken seriously.

"If you're talking about Terry, she's fine," the lieutenant assured him.

"You know Terry?" asked Wynn, somewhat confused.

"I take it by that she hasn't told you yet."

"Told me what?"

"She's been working under cover at Le Club, Mr. Ransome. As has the man you described as watching her. But don't think I don't appreciate your coming in here. Anything at all would be a help with this case."

"Let me get this straight," said Wynn, not sure that what he thought he had heard was correct. "We're talking about Terry Caputo, the interior decorator?"

The lieutenant was starting to smile. "I'm talking about Detective Caputo, one of my best cops."

"Terry's a cop?"

"I'm sure she would have preferred telling you herself. She and Kyle ought to be back any minute."

Wynn stood up. "I'm sorry I troubled you for no reason. I'd better get back to work."

"I just want you to understand, sir, that Terry couldn't tell you. She was ordered not to see you anymore, but she went out to Fire Island despite those orders. However, when the latest strangling happened while you were with her, I lifted that stricture."

Wynn didn't even listen to the lieutenant's explanation. Instead, he turned to the door and there, framing it, were Terry and the man he had suspected of being the strangler.

"What are you doing here?" Terry asked, and her look of surprise turned to one of amusement when the lieutenant spoke from behind Wynn.

"He was worried about you, Terry. Thought something might have happened to you."

Wynn didn't appreciate her amusement. He had been worried, damn it, and she was treating it as some folly of his. Somehow she didn't seem herself at all, and then he realized it was because, for the first time, she *was* being herself. He saw the assurance in the way she carried herself; there was even a look of authority about her he'd never seen before. And it wasn't a uniform that gave her that aura, because she was wearing a plain skirt and blouse, not particularly stylish but suiting her nonetheless.

The thing was, she wasn't apologizing to him; she wasn't making any explanations at all. Instead, she seemed excited about something, and he knew it wasn't about him when she looked past him and said, "We've got an idea, Lieutenant."

"You'll excuse us, won't you?" Lieutenant Corbet said to Wynn. Without another word from Terry, Wynn had the feeling he was being dismissed.

He left the station house in the worst mood of maybe his entire life.

TERRY HAD PUT the problem of Wynn out of her mind, as something she wouldn't have to deal with until later. When, upon entering the squad room, she saw Wynn and divined that "later" had become "now," she was momentarily thrown off balance. She quickly recovered, though, when she saw that Wynn had been thrown more off balance than she.

She knew that here and now was not the time to get into a personal discussion with Wynn. He'd just have to brood about it until she saw him at Le Club. And indeed, "brooding" did seem to describe his face as he left the office.

"Sorry about that, Terry. I figured you had already told him," said the lieutenant, waving them into his office.

"I haven't had a chance."

"Well, I saved you the dramatic scene, then. So what've you got for me?"

"We've been talking," said Terry, looking over at Kyle and waiting for his nod before she went on. "What we think, Lieutenant, is that we should get more preventative at Le Club. My being a decoy sounded like a good idea, but it hasn't worked. What we were thinking is, I'll stay on as a decoy, but Kyle should come out as a cop. Let the women there know we've got some protection for them. I think it would be a good idea for Kyle to talk to the female members who still go, tell them what they should do to protect themselves."

"I have no quarrel with that," said Lieutenant Corbet. "How about the two policewomen I rounded up? Think they'll do?"

Terry opened her mouth and then closed it again, and after a moment Kyle took over.

"They're dogs, Lieutenant."

"Come on, Kyle. They're not that bad," Terry said, interrupting. "It's just that they're not in the kind of shape members of Le Club are in. I swear, Lieutenant, I think the people who go there get in shape first somewhere else."

"In other words, they're fat," said the lieutenant.

Terry started to waffle, saying "Well..."

Kyle said, "Yes, they're fat. The strangler's going to have to be pretty desperate to go from those other women to these. I don't think they'll work as decoys."

"So what do you suggest?" asked the lieutenant.

Terry said, "We think they should be there as cops, too. I know the strangler might not strike again with so many cops around, but isn't that better? It's not as though he's making any mistakes. He could keep killing them and we might never get him. At least this way we might save some lives."

"Whatever you think," said the lieutenant. "But we've only got those policewomen on loan for two weeks maximum. Make the best use of them you can."

LE CLUB HAD A DIFFERENT look that night. When Terry got to the locker room, the female cops were already there. One of them was giving an informal talk to the women who had shown up—and there weren't many of them—and the other was handing out a mimeographed list of do's-and-don't's. One don't was—don't make dates with any men you might meet at Le Club.

"That's the whole point of coming here," one tiny redhead said.

The policewoman said right back to her, "Well, if you think a date is worth dying for, honey, go ahead and be stupid."

There was also posted on the dressing room wall a hotline number that the women could call if they noticed any suspicious behavior on the part of males at Le Club.

Once Terry got to the workout room, though, she didn't think any of the men were going to be acting suspiciously. It was a serious, subdued crowd. Everyone was keeping apart, and even the piped-in music seemed softer.

Kyle was in evidence, and once word got around that he was a cop, he was the only man being flirted with. He had a smug smile on his face, as though he'd known all along that women really went for cops.

Terry didn't see Wynn anywhere. At first it was a relief, although every time she turned around she expected to see him. After a while it became a letdown. She had been prepared for a scene, and now it appeared that he was going to deprive her of one.

Maybe he had already written her off.

It turned out to be a quiet, uneventful evening. When she had finished working out, she and Lisa went out for a quick sandwich, then Terry headed home.

She decided to move the Jeep to the other side of the street rather than have to get up early in the morning to do it, and that was when she found Wynn's note.

She now had his phone number if she wanted to call him, but she wasn't sure she did. Shouldn't he be the one to call? Well, actually, no. She was the one with the explaining to do.

Instead, she found she was busying herself with all kinds of things. She washed out some underwear by hand. She cleaned up the already clean apartment. She thought of watering the plants in the yard, but then remembered it was worth a stiff fine if she was caught doing it, because of the current drought.

After the eleven o'clock news she tried to convince herself that it was too late to call him, but she wasn't successful. Eleven-thirty at night wasn't too late to call any New Yorker.

She dialed his number, heard his voice say hello, then hung up on him. With a shudder, she put down the phone. How childish could she be? She owed him an explanation. She was suddenly acting as skittish as her son had acted on his first date. *Call him,* she kept telling herself. *You've got to call him.*

WYNN WAS PRETTY SURE it was Terry when the phone rang. When the caller hung up on him, he was positive it was she. So she was nervous about talking to him, was she? Well, she had reason to be. It had been pretty thoughtless of her to not return to town like that and have him up most of the night worrying about her. He had even gone so far as to picture her dead, and he never wanted that experience repeated.

He didn't blame her in the least for not telling him she was a cop. She had her orders and she had obeyed them. He could understand that. And he was glad to find out that she wasn't an interior decorator. That had seemed much too mundane a profession for someone like Terry.

He wondered now if the apartment were even hers. Probably not. From what he knew, the police didn't make the kind of money to afford places in that neighborhood.

That left the boat in Brooklyn. If there really was a boat. Perhaps she had gotten it into her head that boats were something all interior decorators had. More likely, she lived in a small apartment there, or maybe even with her family. He had heard it was not at all unusual for unmarried daughters in Italian families to live at home until married. And that would account for her father's phone call.

Hell, for all he knew she could be married. No, that couldn't be possible. Spending the night with him had in no way been part of the job. Of that he was sure.

When the phone rang again, he let it ring three times; then, before she could lose her courage, he answered with, "How are you, Terry?"

There was a pause, then, "Fine, Wynn."

"I'm glad you finally called."

"I didn't see your note until tonight, when I moved the Jeep. But then, you know I wasn't here last night." When he didn't say anything, she said, "I thought I'd see you at the club tonight."

"I wasn't in the mood to work out."

"Hardly anyone was. The place was dead."

"I think they should close it completely."

There was a rather long silence; then she said, "I hope you know I wanted to tell you. I hated having to impersonate a decorator—I don't know the first thing about decorating."

"You'd never know it by your apartment."

"Which isn't mine, as you probably already guessed. Do you mind?"

"Do I mind what, Terry?"

"My being a cop."

"I must admit it takes some getting used to, but it fits. Being an interior decorator never did."

"You probably don't often meet cops."

"I try not to. Usually when people meet police officers, it means they're in trouble of some sort."

"I'm homicide, so you wouldn't be likely to have met me. Unless you killed someone."

"I hadn't planned on it."

There was a silence again, then: "Well, I just wanted to tell you that I hated lying to you."

"Is that all?"

"Yes."

"What about the boat in Brooklyn?"

"What about it?"

"I was just wondering if that was a lie, too."

"No. I do live on a boat in Brooklyn. Not a yacht, you understand—just a cabin cruiser, and nothing great."

Even though his original intention had been to keep her wondering, now he was afraid she was going to hang up with nothing having really been said. "I'm sorry you had to rush off on Saturday."

"No sorrier than I am. I guess you know there had been another murder."

"I read about it in Sunday's paper."

"I suppose I'll see you at Le Club, then. If you're still going, that is."

"Are we allowed to speak?"

"Everyone's seen us speak already, so I don't see why not. But if you see me flirting with any guys, I hope you realize it's the job. And you better not walk me home."

"I guess you were breaking the rules with me, weren't you?"

"I'm afraid so. I want you to know, Wynn, that I never thought it was you. Not for a moment."

"I wouldn't have thought so. I don't think you would've been so stupid as to see me if you had any doubts."

"Well, it's late. I guess I better let you go."

"I haven't forgotten Friday night, Terry. I've missed you."

"I've missed you, too."

When she had hung up, after giving him her phone number, he lay back on the couch and put his feet up. Nothing had really changed except the work she did. It was dangerous work, of course, and he'd probably spend time worrying about her. But that was all right; he'd probably worry about her in any case. And certainly dinner conversation with a homicide detective should prove more interesting than with an interior decorator. She'd probably have some interesting friends, too, although how they'd get along with his friends was a mystery. But then lots of couples had that problem and managed to surmount it.

He found it intriguing that she actually lived on a boat in Brooklyn. That showed the same adventurous spirit that she displayed in her choice of an occupation. It wouldn't be a problem. She worked in the city, and surely she'd see the sense in spending most nights at his place. They could spend occasional weekends on her boat, and the rest of the weekends on Fire Island. They'd have the best of both worlds.

For that matter, she could bring her boat over to Fire Island and dock it there. He'd always thought it would be fun to have a boat on the island. And surely she'd prefer it to Brooklyn.

The natural thing would be for her to invite him out to her boat for the weekend now that there were no secrets between them. It would be a nice change from Fire Island, and this time maybe they'd get to spend the entire weekend together.

At any rate, he was glad she was safe, not upset at all that she was a cop. Everything looked as though it was going to turn out fine after all—in fact, even better than he'd ever supposed. He never had been crazy about interior decorators.

TERRY MARCHED into the lieutenant's office the next morning and said, "Is there any reason why I have to still be a blonde? Obviously I didn't appeal to him as a blonde or he wouldn't have gone for a brunette last time."

Lieutenant Corbet grinned. "Other than the fact that you went to all the trouble to bleach it and you look stunning, no."

Terry grinned back at him. "Good, because I'm sick of it. Do you know blondes get talked to on the street?"

"Not being a blonde, I wouldn't know."

"Well, I do. All kinds of guys make remarks to me, and they're usually prefaced with 'blondie.'"

"I can see where that would be annoying."

"I also get whistled at."

"You're a good-looking woman, Terry."

"I didn't get whistled at as a brunette."

"I'm sure you got your share."

She sat down across from him and folded her arms. "No, there's a difference. Brunettes get respect; blondes get hassled. Could I take an hour off this afternoon and get it dyed back?"

"Take all the time you want, but won't it look strange your showing up with a different hair color tonight?"

She shook her head decisively. "Not at all. Some of the women there appear to change hair color weekly. And as of this moment, blond is not the most popular color at Le Club."

"So how'd it go last night?"

"There aren't many women who still go there, but I think the policewomen were effective. The female members who are still going seem to be taking the danger seriously."

"How'd Kyle do?"

Terry smiled. "As the only safe man there, he had the women all over him."

"In his glory, huh?"

She nodded. "When it's over, Lieutenant... What I mean is, will Kyle and I still be members?"

"I imagine something could be arranged. If we solve the case, that is. Otherwise, I don't think there'll be a Le Club much longer. You like it there, do you?"

"I love it. They've got the best equipment I've ever seen."

"Was Sanger there last night?"

"Would you be if your girlfriend had just been killed?"

"He's off the hook. And the MO came in the same." Then he leaned back in his chair, putting it at a dangerous angle, and said, "You know something, Terry? I'm going to miss you as a blonde."

"Go to hell," muttered Terry, then added, "sir."

"I DON'T KNOW, honey," the hairdresser said. "If you dye it dark again, every time you shampoo it's going to get a little lighter. Probably turn some odd colors in the process."

"It's better than letting it grow out," Terry insisted. "First of all, it'll take years, and second of all, I don't fancy going around with dark roots."

"I say let's cut it all off."

Terry glared at him in the mirror. Sure, what did he care? He was almost bald. "It took me ten years to get it this long," she informed him.

"It doesn't suit you."

"It's not always sticking out like this. Usually I keep it in a braid."

"Trust me."

"Oh, what the hell—cut it off. But make it some haircut that doesn't take any time." It wasn't that she trusted him at all, but it did seem the easiest way. Anyway, the reason she had let her hair grow long to begin with was because Nick had liked long hair. As far as she was concerned, short hair would be a lot easier to dry every morning.

When he had finished cutting it and dyeing it and drying it under heat lamps, she rather liked the way it looked. It wasn't that different from the way she looked with her hair in a braid, except for more softness around the face.

"Just one thing," she said to the hairdresser.

"Yes?" he said, as though questioning her taste.

"I want the eyebrows darkened again."

"Of course. I was going to suggest it myself."

Back at the station everyone pretended not to recognize her, but then one of them yelled out, "Hey, it's Rainkisser, and she's got a new look."

Terry could really have done without police humor.

THAT NIGHT LISA wasn't at Le Club, nor was Wynn. The place had in fact lost a lot of its charm. There was virtually no banter between the sexes, and it seemed to Terry that the only ones there were the serious bodybuilders and the cops.

The only one who even noticed her new hair color was Scott, and he did a double take when she walked into the workout area. As she walked by him, he stopped her by saying, "Is she or isn't she? Only her hairdresser knows."

"Recognized me, huh?" Terry said, not liking the feeling of being the kind of woman who changed the color of her hair on a whim.

"I like it dark," Scott replied. "That your natural color?"

She nodded.

"It looks good. I personally think blondes are highly overrated."

That remark made her night. She just hoped Wynn felt the same way.

She was up to three miles on the track now and feeling pretty good about it. She was even thinking of going in for marathons and maybe getting Mike interested in running. Although where they'd run in Mill Basin, she didn't know.

All the way home she was half expecting to see Wynn waiting for her when she got there. She was disappointed when her block was empty and sorry she hadn't stopped for something to eat.

She called Mike and checked in on him, then called Pop, got Cindi instead, and made the conversation brief. Tony wasn't using the boat yet; at the moment he was posting signs around and doing some advertising for his fishing business.

By nine o'clock, with nothing to watch on television but repeats, she was beginning to be so bored she was thinking of calling Kathy. Instead, Wynn called.

"How'd it go tonight?" he asked her, and she told him how dead the club had been.

"I can't believe this guy's killed so many women and is still walking around."

"I know; it's frightening. But it's always hard to catch this kind of killer because there's no obvious motive."

"Why don't you fingerprint every male member and employee?"

"Because the killer hasn't left any prints."

"I guess you would've thought of that. It makes me feel helpless. I wish I could do something."

"If you feel helpless, how do you think we feel?"

"Are you allowed to see me?"

"Sure. Just not at Le Club. And if some guy should try to pick me up there, I'll have to leave with him. Not that that seems likely anymore."

"Has that happened yet?"

Terry debated whether to tell him, then decided there were enough lies between them. "Yeah, one night. A guy named Craig." She told him what happened, and he said, "Sounds like a perfectly normal guy to me."

"You know something, Wynn? It's a lot easier talking to you now. I used to have to watch everything I said."

"I noticed."

"I figured you did. It's hard, though. Pretend being someone else for a day and see how scintillating you are."

"You had your moments."

"Yeah?"

"Oh, yes."

"But I wasn't doing any talking, was I?"

"Not that I could notice."

Damn, when was she going to see him again? "I've got another surprise for you, Wynn."

"Let's hear it."

"I'm not a blonde anymore. So, if you're partial to blondes..."

"Do you have short hair?"

"How'd you know that?"

"Don't you remember those drawings I did of you? Even then I saw you with short, dark hair."

"I'd forgotten. Well, that's what I look like now." And she wondered if subconsciously she had remembered and was now trying to please Wynn as she had Nick. She didn't think so, though; she had gotten over being like some guy's image of her a long time ago.

Wynn was saying, "Now I understand why you didn't jump at the chance to model. I guess your job must be pretty exciting."

"Some of the time. The rest of the time it's as boring as any other job."

"So how about tomorrow night? You want to see where I live?"

"Are you trying to get me over to your place to seduce me?"

"If that's a prerequisite, then yes."

"You're on."

"You can leave your gun at home."

She chuckled. "I never leave my gun at home."

"You mean you've always had it with you?"

"Of course. Does that bother you?"

"I imagine I'll get used to it," he said, then told her he'd see her at the club the following night.

Terry loved the sound of that—that he'd get used to it. It must mean he didn't mind her being a cop. In fact, if she wasn't mistaken, he seemed to find her more interesting as a cop, which didn't surprise her, as she'd had nothing to talk about as an interior decorator.

Of course, it remained to be seen if he'd find her interesting as a mother.

Chapter Ten

Wynn owned a co-op in one of the new buildings near Lincoln Center. Terry was impressed by just the lobby and the elevator. Her initial impression of his apartment was that it was larger than it actually was, but that was because everything was so neat, with everything in its proper place. The apartment was all done in browns and off-whites—the furniture oak, the few paintings on the walls modern. The focal point of the living room was the enormous window, with a view of Lincoln Center spread out below.

He showed her around. There was a small but well-equipped kitchen that looked unused; there was a large master bedroom with a separate bath and another smaller room that he used as a study.

She couldn't help thinking that Mike and a large dog wouldn't fit in at all there, even if the building did allow children and dogs, which she doubted.

He came up behind her as she was looking at the view and put his hands on her shoulders. "What do you think?"

"It's very nice."

His hands moved to her waist and he pulled her back against him. "The decorator said he was trying for a subtly masculine flavor."

"He succeeded," she said, thinking that now she knew what was missing. It did look like the apartment of a man; a solitary man.

"I like being able to walk across the street to the concerts. And Columbus Avenue has some good restaurants."

She had read about Columbus Avenue, the new gathering place of the yuppies. Still, she wasn't critical like some people. She thought fixing up bad neighborhoods could only benefit the city.

He said, "I don't have any food in the house, but we could order up Chinese if you want."

The feel of his body against hers was making her think of anything but food. "I'm not particularly hungry."

"Would you like a drink?"

She moved around to face him, and before she could say no to the drink, his mouth was covering hers. When they broke apart he said, "I guess we could eat later."

She said, "Yes, later," and then he was leading her into his bedroom.

This time they made love more slowly, taking more care, and in the light of the setting sun she was able to see the loving look in his eyes as they explored each other's bodies. His was slimmer than Nick's had been, harder, the muscle coordination better. Nick's had had more body hair, which she remembered had excited her. And where Nick's young exuberance had proved both exhausting and fulfilling, Wynn's greater mastery brought an equal sense of fulfillment.

Afterward, he said, "Will you spend the night?"

"I can't. I wish I could. Until the case is solved, I don't think I better."

"You're nowhere near solving it, are you?"

She shook her head. "We just can't figure any motive."

"Maybe they wouldn't go to bed with him."

"You kill someone for that?"

Wynn raised his hands. "I don't."

"You've probably never been rejected."

He turned on the bedside lamp and looked at her. "You really believe that?"

"I don't see you denying it."

He chuckled. "I don't plan on denying it. If you think I'm that irresistible, who am I to argue?"

That didn't deserve an answer, so she said, "None of it adds up. First he kills all blondes, now he's switched to a brunette. And he never leaves a clue."

"It's like you," he observed.

"What's like me?"

"You didn't add up, either, but now that I know you're a cop, the pieces begin to fit together."

Terry was suddenly reminded that there were still pieces he didn't have a clue about.

Once again he seemed to be reading her mind. "I'd like to see that boat of yours," he said, not waiting for an invitation.

"It's nothing much, Wynn."

"It's your home."

"Well, the only time I go out there at the moment is the weekends, and you're on Fire Island then."

"Would you rather come out to the island with me this weekend?"

"No, I can't."

He was quiet then and she knew there was no reason why he should understand when she hadn't told him anything he could understand. She thought of the problems involved with taking him home to Brooklyn with her, but putting it off wouldn't solve any of them. "You want to come out there with me this weekend?" she asked with reluctance, but not with as much reluctance as she was actually feeling.

"Only if you really want me to."

"Don't play coy, Wynn—you practically forced me into inviting you."

He moved his head so that his lips were against her neck. "I know. I didn't mean to force things, but I don't feel like spending another weekend not seeing you."

"All right. We'll go out after workout Friday. I don't come back in until Monday morning, though. Is that okay with you?"

"Do I bring my yachting clothes?"

"Sure, if you want to be laughed out of the marina."

He rolled partially on top of her and said, "You want to get something to eat before I send you home in a cab?"

Her arms went around him. "No, thanks."

"Is there anything you want before I send you home in a cab?"

"What do you think?" she asked, pulling him on top of her.

"I think we're in total agreement."

THE NEXT MORNING Terry busied herself with paperwork, reports that had been piling up. No matter how she tried to concentrate on her job, though, thoughts of Wynn kept fogging up her mind. It was a nice fog, but it began to clear when she thought of the weekend ahead.

First of all, she was going to have to warn Mike. She should have brought up the subject of Wynn with him long ago, but something her son said always prevented it. She was going to bring home a totally unexpected man, and she didn't think that would go over well with Mike.

She didn't think Pop would be a problem. Pop could hardly complain when he had moved Cindi in with him. And heaven only knew what Wynn would think of Cindi.

It was too early to call Mike, who was still in school, but she dialed Kathy's number, wanting to get someone's opinion of the situation.

"You're getting a man and I'm losing one" was Kathy's only comment.

"I haven't got him, Kath, nor have you lost Johnny. Unless something's happened that I haven't heard about."

"I went to a lawyer."

"Oh, Kath..."

"Not for a divorce, for a legal separation. I want it down in writing that Johnny's going to pay child support."

"Johnny wouldn't stop supporting the kids."

"You never know what might happen. He's under that woman's spell and she could convince him of anything."

"Have you talked to him?"

"Not a word, but the kids call him. Also, I got a job, Terry."

"That's great."

"It's just part-time, at the parish. Mostly I answer the phone and listen to people's problems."

That wasn't much better than watching soaps, Terry thought, although maybe other people's problems would take Kathy's mind off her own. As for her own problem...

"How do you think Mike'll react when I bring Wynn home?" Terry asked her.

"That's hard to say. Have you told him anything about Wynn?"

"Worse. Neither of them knows of the other's existence."

"I'd like to be there to see this."

"Not this weekend, please. I think Wynn's going to have to contend with enough with just Pop and Mike. And Cindi, of course."

"Where's he going to sleep, Terry? If you want to send Mike over to my place, you're welcome to."

"I think that would be worse. I'd be throwing him out of his home and replacing him with Wynn."

"Yeah, I guess. That's going to be pretty cozy, the three of you there. I'm dying to meet him, you know."

"I know and I'm dying to have you meet him." That was something of an exaggeration. "Maybe on the Fourth we could have a family picnic and he could meet everyone. If I'm still seeing him by then."

"Things aren't going well?"

"They couldn't be better, except that he still knows virtually nothing about me except that I'm a cop."

"Lots of luck."

"Thanks."

Terry put off calling Mike for the rest of the day. She decided she needed privacy to talk to him, which was hard to get at work. But it was guilt, she knew, more than anything else. She should have prepared him; he wasn't going to understand her just showing up with a strange man.

Maybe she should put Wynn off. She could call him and tell him this weekend wasn't good and instead make plans for him to visit the following weekend. Not that she couldn't still do that if the phone call with Mike didn't go over well. Now that she had invited Wynn, she was looking forward to having him around for the weekend. And thinking about it wasn't going to solve anything. The only thing that would was talking to Mike.

Wynn was working late on his new ad campaign. Ralph Lauren had cornered the market on the preppies; the yuppies had discovered The Banana Republic and were big these days on the "safari" look. That left the normal people in the country, who were the ones Wynn had wanted to appeal to in the first place.

Terry was his idea of normal. The trouble was, Terry wasn't interested in clothes. And maybe that's what made people normal, the fact that they weren't trying to portray an image.

So how did he get people like that to buy his clothes?

It wasn't any good pushing the natural fiber thing because none of the good manufacturers were using synthetics these days. His clothes were designed for comfort, but they weren't unique in that way. Cashing in on the fitness craze, lots of designers were going for comfort.

He was still convinced that the way to go was with a totally new look in models. There must be a whole lot of women in the country who were sick and tired of the skinny, ethereal creatures who were forever being paraded before their eyes in the fashion magazines. Not that he intended to use fat models. Not only didn't they look good in his clothes, but he didn't even make his things in large sizes.

What he wanted was normal-looking women of average size. Women like Terry. Women who would appeal to all the other women just like them. Women who would see his ads and think, "I really could look like that."

No, that wasn't what he wanted. What he really wanted was for Terry to model for his ads. But maybe that was love talking and not business sense. Still, it wouldn't hurt to ask her again.

TERRY PUT OFF calling Mike until late Friday afternoon. And then, when he wasn't home, she called her father.

"He went to the beach with his friends," he told her.

"On a school day?"

"They got out yesterday, Terry. Haven't you talked to him lately?"

"Listen, Pop—I've been seeing a man."

"I figured. And may I say, it's about time, Terry."

"The thing is, I've invited him to the boat for the weekend."

"Want him to meet Mike, huh?"

"He doesn't even know about Mike."

"I assume you're going to tell him before they meet face-to-face."

Terry sighed. "Of course I am, but I want to prepare Mike, too. How do you think he'll take it?"

"That's hard to say. But it wouldn't be a bad thing for Mike to have a father. Or for you to have a husband, for that matter."

"Please don't say anything like that this weekend, Pop. I've hardly even known him very long."

"Long enough to spend the night with him, I gather."

"I don't want any lectures, Pop."

"And you aren't going to get one." He sounded insulted, which was a big sham.

"Have Mike call me when he gets back, okay? And let me be the one to tell him about it."

By the time Mike did call, which was right when she was supposed to be leaving work, she was a nervous wreck. She was sure she understood exactly how cheating spouses felt when they had to confess. And why she was allowing a twelve-year-old to put her into such a state of panic she didn't know, except that it had been just the two of them for so long and she didn't know how Mike could help being jealous.

She tried to think how to ease gently into the subject, couldn't come up with anything and finally said, "I'm bringing a friend home for the weekend, honey."

"Well, I hope she doesn't mind getting fleas. I don't know where Henry got them, but they're all over the boat and he's been sleeping in your bunk."

Somehow she couldn't imagine Wynn with fleas and smiled at the thought. "It's a man, Mike."

There was a long silence.

"I met him at the health club I told you about. He's very nice and he wanted to see our boat."

Still silence.

"I think you'll like him."

"You mean you like him and you hope I will." He sounded sullen, which wasn't like him. But then, it wasn't like her to bring a man home.

"I do like him."

"Where's he going to sleep?"

"I was hoping Tony left his futon there."

"Yeah, he did. Do I have to sleep in it?"

She had been about to suggest just that, but now she said, "Of course not. I wouldn't make you give up your bunk. I'm sure Wynn's slept on the floor before." On second thought, she wasn't at all sure.

"I never heard of a guy named Wynn."

"Don't judge him by his name, Mike. Wait until you meet him." When he didn't reply, she said, "Do I give you a hard time about your friends?"

"You did about Manny. You said he was a bad influence."

Leave it to him to remember the one exception. "Yes, and Manny's in reform school now and you aren't. And if you want to discuss your shoplifting days, Mike, that's fine with me."

"Once. One time."

"You mean you only got caught one time."

"All right, Mom. I'll be polite to your friend."

"Please don't be polite, Mike. I know how you are when you're polite. Just be yourself, okay?"

"Okay."

"See you later, honey."

"See you, Mom."

One hurdle crossed. Now all she had to do was tell Wynn.

TERRY AND WYNN left for Brooklyn directly from Le Club. Telling Wynn about Mike was hanging heavily over her head, but despite that, she chattered on and on about the case until finally she realized they were in Brooklyn. It was still a long drive out to Mill Basin, but she knew she had better start preparing him.

She glanced over at Wynn. He was wearing topsiders and jeans that looked as though they'd been cleaned and pressed, and a shirt with a reptile over the pocket, which would make him the best-dressed man at the marina. She hoped he'd brought along shorts, or at least an old pair of jeans.

"You know," she said to him, "there are things you don't know about me."

He reached over and rested a hand on her thigh. "There's a lot you don't know about me, too. We'll have to do some talking this weekend."

That would be nice, but there wasn't much chance of it. She couldn't think of any way to lead into it gently, so she just blurted out the words. "I have a son."

Her eyes were looking straight ahead and she could feel her palms begin to sweat on the steering wheel. She thought maybe he was waiting for more, so she said, "He's twelve. He lives on the boat with me."

"I've wondered about you," he said, "but the possibility of your having children never occurred to me."

"If it makes you feel any better, he didn't know about you until today, either."

"Why should you think you have to make me feel better about it?"

"I should've told you before."

"Why didn't you?"

She stole a quick glance at him to see how he was taking it. He was staring straight ahead, his face showing no emotion at all. "If you want me to take you home, Wynn, I will."

His grip tightened on her thigh, then relaxed. Ignoring her offer, he said, "I understand that you had to lie to me before, and we never did talk much about ourselves personally. What'd your son have to say about it?"

"He wasn't thrilled."

"Well, you can stop worrying about me. The feeling isn't mutual."

"I'm sure he'll like you when he meets you. It's just that I've never dated before."

"Never dated?"

"Not since his father died."

"I must've done something right."

"Or maybe I was just ready."

They rode in silence for a few minutes, then he said, "How long have you been a widow?"

"Seven years."

"If you'd rather not talk about it..."

"I don't mind, Wynn. He was a cop, too—he was killed. I'd been on the force before Mike was born, and after Nick died I went back. Nick and I grew up together—married when we were both nineteen."

He reached over and ruffled her short hair, something he tended to do a lot since she'd cut it. "Did you think I'd mind that you're a widow with a son?"

"I didn't know," she answered truthfully. "Do you?"

"Not at all, although it looks like we're not going to have any privacy this weekend."

"Probably not."

"On the other hand, it should be interesting."

EVERY TIME HE THOUGHT he was finally getting her in perspective, he learned something new about her. He liked the idea of her having a son. For the most part, the women he knew didn't want children; they were more interested in maintaining their figures than in motherhood. And he'd never given any real thought to having children of his own.

A daughter might have been easier than a son. A son would be sure to resent him. Well, maybe not. Being Terry's son, he was probably an interesting child. Besides, Wynn had always gotten along with children the few times he had been around them. He treated them as equals and they liked that.

He wondered if she had gotten over the death of her husband. Well, if she hadn't, it was about time she did. Certainly he hadn't sensed any ghost between them when they made love.

Terry was saying something to him and he hadn't been paying attention. "What was that?"

"I asked you how old you are."

"Thirty-five."

"I thought you were around my age. I'll be thirty-four in September."

She continued to surprise him. Any other woman would have lied about her age, and certainly she could get away with it. Or at least have hung on to thirty-three as long as possible. But then, as he had learned, she wasn't like any of the other women he knew.

She said, "You're awfully quiet all of a sudden."

"I was just thinking."

"Well, don't think. Talk to me. I'm nervous enough as it is."

"It's pretty around here. I didn't realize Brooklyn would have neighborhoods of big houses."

"What'd you expect?"

"Truthfully?"

"Of course."

"I guess I expected tenements."

She laughed. "Brooklyn has its share of those. But there are lots of neighborhoods like this, too. And then there are places like Sheepshead Bay, which looks like a New England fishing town."

"Don't you mind the long drive twice a day?"

"Sometimes. But most of the time it feels good to get out of Manhattan."

"You don't enjoy living in that sublet?"

She turned to him with a grin. "Actually, in ways I do. It's the first time I've ever lived alone. But I wouldn't want to do it on a long-term basis."

He knew she was referring to her son, but hoped that she also might mean she wouldn't be averse to living with a man again. Except living together would no doubt be out of the question with a twelve-year-old son. Some women might do it, but he didn't think Terry was one of them. No, for her it would have to be marriage, he was sure.

Marriage didn't necessarily present a problem. Wynn had nothing against marriage if it was to Terry. He had had a hard time imagining it with any of the other women he had known, but the prospect of marriage to Terry seemed right. It would also please his mother no end. He knew she wondered why, with the good example his parents had set for him, he himself had never married.

They had reached a newer-looking area with rows of two-family brick houses, the front of each boasting a small, well-kept yard.

"This is Mill Basin," she told him. "We're almost there."

She drove past a small shopping center, then turned in to a parking lot and stopped the Jeep. "We're here," she said, and seemed to be hesitant to get out of the Jeep.

He got out and took his canvas bag out of the back, then looked out over the marina, where the sun was getting ready to set.

"Just one thing," said Terry, finally getting out to join him. "Be prepared for anything."

Evidently she was more nervous than he was about the coming meeting with her son.

He admired some of the boats as they walked down the dock. There were several cabin cruisers and two large sailboats, plus a number of smaller boats. He always liked the smell of the salt water, and the air out here seemed fresh and clean. He could hear rock music being played on one of the boats and wondered if that was Mike.

He was following her, and when she stopped in front of one of the smaller cabin cruisers, he waited for her to jump on board, then followed suit. Fortunately his leap didn't seem too clumsy to him. She had been so adept at it that he would have felt foolish to have skidded aboard.

And then, without any forewarning at all, a huge, brown blur leaped at him, and the next thing he knew he was flying off the deck and plunging into the water.

Chapter Eleven

"What was that, Mom?" asked Mike, coming on deck just in time to hear the splash. "You drop something overboard?"

"That was Wynn," she told him, watching the water as Wynn's familiar head surfaced. "You okay?" she yelled down at him, knowing there was no point in her jumping in after him since he was a much better swimmer than she was.

He was treading water now and looking rather lost. "I was attacked by something," he said.

"Bad Henry," murmured Terry, looking down at the happy dog, still wagging his tail in greeting. "I'm afraid that was Henry. He gets excited when we have visitors."

"Henry?"

She pulled Henry over to the side of the boat so that Wynn could see him. "Our dog."

"I see. How do I get back up there?"

"If you swim around to the other side, you'll see a ladder." She turned to Mike. "How about jumping in and rescuing his bag, since you're in your bathing suit anyway. I think he forgot about his clothes."

Mike dove in, retrieved the bag, and was right behind Wynn when he climbed up the ladder. She could see Pop and Cindi coming out on the deck of Pop's boat, both of them staring with interest at the soaking Wynn, who was quickly forming a puddle on the deck.

"How you folks doing?" yelled Pop.

Wynn mumbled something about nosy neighbors, getting a chuckle out of Mike. "Those aren't neighbors," said Mike. "That's my grandpa and his girlfriend."

"Did you bring along a bathing suit?" Terry asked Wynn.

He nodded, then opened his bag. "My shorts are only slightly damp," he said. "I'll change into them."

She headed for the cabin, telling him to follow. She pointed out the bathroom to him and said, "Bring up your wet things after you're dressed and I'll lay them out on the deck to dry."

Henry, who had followed them down, was now wriggling with joy in front of Wynn.

"You didn't mention a dog," he told her.

"I forgot. Somehow, after a son, a dog didn't seem that important."

"At least your son didn't push me overboard."

She smiled. "Henry didn't mean to. Look at him, he's crazy about you already."

Wynn smiled at that, and she didn't mention that Henry loved everyone. That knocked him out of the category of watchdog, but made him wonderful with people.

She went back up on deck and saw that Pop and Cindi were still outside. "Bring him over for a drink,"

Pop called out, and she figured why not?—he was going to have to meet them sometime.

"We'll be over in a little while."

Mike was looking as though he felt left out, and she put an arm around him.

He shook it off, which was normal behavior, and said, "What're we going to eat?"

"Why is that always your first question?"

"Because I'm always hungry when you get home. But if you want another question, what happened to your hair?"

"I had it cut off."

"I could see that. Get tired of being a blonde?"

"It's hard work being a blonde, Mike. You want to go over to Sal's and bring home some pizza?"

"Sure. Two be enough?"

"Get three—we'll take them over to your grandpa's."

"Shouldn't I stick around and meet that guy first?"

"You can meet me now," said Wynn, coming up the steps and looking much more "Mill Basin" in shorts and a T-shirt, his feet bare. "I'm Wynn Ransome," he said, holding out his hand to Mike.

Mike shook hands with him, asking, "Any preference in pizza?"

"None," said Wynn, which sounded to Terry as though he didn't like any kind, but since she didn't see any alternative, she didn't question it. He'd have to go through a lot worse than eating pizza over the weekend anyway, she had a feeling.

WYNN DIDN'T MIND Terry's boat, although it seemed awfully small and crowded for two people and a large dog. Her father's boat, though, was great. The cabin was furnished like a living room with sliding glass doors out to the deck, and he could see through a doorway to a large bedroom. This, he thought, was the way to live on a boat.

He liked her father right off. The guy was too good-looking and charming for his own good, but his handshake was firm and his eyes friendly when he welcomed Wynn on board.

The girlfriend was something else. She seemed very young and giggled a lot, and if Wynn had passed the two of them on the street, he would have taken her for his granddaughter. Well, daughter, anyway. He didn't look old enough to be a grandfather, even though Wynn knew he was. He was totally different from Wynn's own father, who had turned prematurely gray at thirty and whose idea of sport clothes had been loosening his tie when he got home from work.

Wynn was offered a beer and accepted, and then they sat around making small talk until Mike returned with the pizzas. Wynn knew that pizza was popular with just about everybody, but he'd never acquired a taste for it. He guessed it was all a matter of what you grew up with; in his parents' house it would have been considered junk food. In the middle of eating the pizza, as though on cue, they all turned to the television set, and Terry's father got up and put it on.

"You a Mets fan?" Mike asked him when the ball game was tuned in.

"I don't follow baseball," Wynn told him.

For some reason he was suddenly the center of attention. "You don't like baseball?" asked Terry's father.

"Not particularly."

He saw Mike glance at his mother as though she'd suddenly gone off the deep end, but he'd be damned if he was going to tell lies to ingratiate himself with her family. They'd have to accept him for what he was or not at all. It wasn't that he didn't understand the game; he had played it in school like everyone else. It was just that he found watching it boring.

"What kind of work do you do, Wynn?" asked her father.

"I design and manufacture women's clothing."

There was a hushed silence, fortunately broken when the Mets scored, but then, after a few comments on the game, all eyes again turned to him.

"Well, I think that's real interesting," Cindi said. But since she found just about everything interesting, no one paid any attention to her.

"It's a living," said Wynn, trying to downplay it.

"You make a lot of money doing that?" Mike asked him, then said, after he was given a nudge by Terry, "What's the matter, aren't I supposed to ask that?"

"That's not polite, Mike," said Terry's father.

Mike immediately said, "But Mom told me not to be polite."

Wynn looked at Terry, and she shrugged and said, "I just didn't want him acting unnatural, that's all."

"You look real cute with short hair," Cindi said to Terry, but everyone ignored her.

Between watching a game that bored him to death and being questioned during every commercial break, Wynn thought the evening would never end.

It didn't improve when they returned to Terry's boat and he found he was going to sleep on a futon. On the deck. Alone.

He couldn't remember going through such an experience since high school, when the fathers of the girls he dated always put him through a question-and-answer period when he picked up their daughters for dates. He decided that one of the benefits of living in New York was that all the women he had dated had lived alone, their families usually in other states.

He didn't have anything against families in general or Terry's in particular. It was just that they made him feel like an adolescent, which wasn't a great feeling. Still, they were warm and friendly and very affectionate with each other, which he admired. His relatives were more the type to shake hands than to hug or kiss.

He wondered what it would feel like to be part of such a family and decided it would feel good. They seemed to yell and argue a lot, but it was all done in a way that he knew meant they loved and cared about each other at the same time. This was also something he wasn't used to in his own life, but he'd much rather be yelled at or argued with than be given the silent treatment or treated politely but coolly.

There'd be problems with Mike, but that was to be expected. He figured there'd be problems with any man the kid's mother got interested in, short of maybe the shortstop for the Mets, whom Mike appeared to adore. And if getting close to Mike required Wynn to summon up an interest in baseball, well, it could have been worse. The kid could have been one of those computer game freaks, which would have driven Wynn nuts.

He felt the deck sway and looked up to see a dark presence looming over him. This time he was prepared, though, and when Henry lay down, Wynn moved to the side so that he wasn't covered by the dog.

"Good dog," he said, patting Henry on the head.

A wet tongue on his face told him his feelings were reciprocated.

"WHAT'RE YOU DOING TODAY?" Terry asked Mike the next morning.

"Nothing."

"You're not seeing your friends?"

"I thought I'd just hang around."

"Look, Mike, I don't need chaperoning. I also need to clean this place up, so why don't you take Wynn out in the rowboat? Maybe you could do some fishing."

"He fishes?" Mike asked, sounding doubtful.

"If he doesn't, he can learn."

"Yeah, okay." He seemed very reluctant.

"If you don't want to, you can stay and help me clean."

"I'll take him. Do we get breakfast first?"

"Make up the bunks while I fix it, okay?"

Wynn didn't look as if he had slept well when he came down to breakfast. That surprised her. She always slept like a log in the fresh air.

The day turned out to be pretty good. Wynn didn't seem to mind going fishing with Mike, and she was able to give the boat a good cleaning. Then she went to the supermarket and picked up steaks for dinner in case they didn't catch anything. When she returned they were back, and between them they had six fish, which she decided to save until Sunday.

She sent Mike off on an errand to the drugstore and asked, "How did it go?"

"He talks a lot when you get him alone."

"Yeah. Sometimes he doesn't shut up."

"That's okay. I was afraid he'd want to discuss baseball."

"How'd you grow up without liking baseball?"

"I liked it when I was a kid. It just seems kind of childish now."

She hoped he kept that opinion from Pop. And the rest of the men in her family. "Mike usually goes out with his friends on Saturday nights, but I have a feeling he's planning on staying home and keeping an eye on us," she warned Wynn.

He nodded. "I got the same feeling."

"You want to take him to a movie tonight?"

"I wouldn't mind going to a movie."

"I better warn you—it'll be science fiction."

"We can't outvote him?"

"Only one problem. If we take him to anything else, he'll say 'barf' every time it gets serious. I see a lot of science fiction movies."

"It's better than baseball," said Wynn.

The movie could have been worse, but not much. Mike insisted on sitting between them in the theater, and whenever Terry looked over to see how Wynn was doing, he appeared to be trying to stay awake.

When they got home, Terry took two folding chairs up on deck, and Mike, apparently convinced that nothing was going to happen out in the open, went down to the cabin and went to bed.

"Not quite like a weekend on Fire Island, I'm afraid," Terry said.

"Not anything like one."

"I'm sorry. You must be having a miserable time."

"Not at all. It's quite different from the island, but interesting in its own way."

"If he gets to know you, it won't be like this. He's usually with his friends on the weekends."

He reached out and took her hand. "But I'd say the affair is over, wouldn't you?"

She had the awful feeling he was ending it. "If you want," she said.

"I'm not talking about not seeing you anymore, Terry. I just mean that it's not likely we're going to be able to be alone together once the case is solved. Unless you stayed at my place in the city occasionally."

"I couldn't. I'd feel as if I were sneaking around on him."

There wasn't much to say about it after that, and when she caught Wynn yawning, she stood up and said, "I'll see you in the morning."

"You going to bed already?"

"I want to get up for early Mass."

A silence, then; "I'll go with you."

"Are you Catholic?"

"No. But I'd still like to go."

She leaned down and gave him a kiss. "I'll wake you in the morning, then. I hope you sleep better tonight."

"Henry kept licking my face."

She burst out laughing. "Yes, he does that. I'll keep him in the cabin tonight."

"That's okay. If I can't have you, I'll settle for Henry."

TERRY HAD A SHOCK in store for her when they returned from Mass. She knew as soon as she saw Kathy's car in the parking lot that her sister had ignored her advice and come over anyway. What she wasn't prepared for was Kathy dressed head to foot in WIN clothing.

"Hi," yelled Kathy, on the deck of Pop's boat, as soon as they came into view.

"I don't believe this," Terry muttered.

Wynn seemed equally surprised. "Who's my walking advertisement?"

"My sister. And I assure you, she's never worn your clothing before."

"Well, don't knock her for having good taste," Wynn teased.

Kathy seemed beside herself at being introduced to her idea of a celebrity, and her teenage daughter was looking at Wynn as if he were a movie star.

That was bad enough, but an hour later, Tony, who just happened to pick that day to take the aunts for a ride, showed up with his kids, Joanna, and aunts Rosa and Anna. All of which took a certain talent, since Tony drove a compact car.

Tony immediately launched into his plans for charter fishing, for some reason trying to get Wynn's approval. Aunt Anna invited him over for a home-cooked meal, and Aunt Rosa drew her cards out of her sleeve and asked if Wynn would like a reading.

Terry, wanting to change into something more comfortable, went over to her own boat and left him to sink or swim.

AUNT ROSA WAS TELLING his fortune with the tarot cards. Already she had gotten out of him that he was an Aries, and had made some remark to the effect that an Aries and a Libra were exceptionally compatible, which led him to believe that either Terry was a Libra or Aunt Rosa was, and that she was actually flirting with him. He wouldn't mind, though; he was quite taken with her, too.

The other aunt—he couldn't remember her name—was hovering over them, her mustache almost twitching with excitement. She kept saying things like, "Oh, yes, good fortune," and, "Oh, yes, long life," until Aunt Rosa finally told her to quit interrupting.

Mike was talking to his cousins, and from the way they kept glancing at him, he was sure he was the prime topic of conversation. Terry's sister was striking different poses in his clothing, which he found embarrassing. So far he hadn't mentioned them and neither had she, and he hoped it stayed that way.

He didn't know why he had ever thought regular women would make better models for his clothes than professional models. Here was a certainly normal woman, but he had to admit that while she might look comfortable in his clothes, anyone seeing her wouldn't rush out to buy them.

It bothered him that he couldn't figure out why she didn't look good in them. Other than being heavier and having her hair frosted, she didn't look all that different from Terry. And yet he knew Terry would look great in them. Or maybe, as was said, love really was blind.

Terry's brother was the hyper sort who had bent his ear nonstop about some charter-fishing venture he was starting. Wynn had heard enough about fishing for the day and had successfully tuned him out.

He hadn't minded going fishing with Mike. It was just that his idea of fishing wasn't sitting in a rowboat and waiting interminably for the fish to bite. He had always enjoyed deep-sea fishing, but that was more for the companionship involved than the actual sport.

Mike's idea of companionship had been to relate every funny incident that had occurred in his classroom during the entire school year. He had also told Wynn several jokes, all of which Wynn had heard when he was in grade school.

But the boy was okay. He looked like Terry, which right away had been a plus in his favor. What the boy thought of him, though, was a mystery.

How he was ever going to get Terry alone was also a mystery. Obviously he could invite her out to Fire Island for the following weekend, but he'd have to invite Mike, too. And since Mike wouldn't know anyone out there, he'd be with them every minute. And he and Terry wouldn't be able to share a bedroom with Mike along.

The same went for his Manhattan apartment. And there was more of a problem there, since the building didn't allow children or dogs. And he was pretty sure that getting Terry on any permanent basis would be a package deal that would naturally include Mike and almost certainly Henry.

He had forgiven Henry for shoving him into the water. Henry, ugly as he was, was an exceptionally lovable dog. He could get used very quickly to having Henry around. His clothes would take a beating, of course, but he'd give up sartorial elegance for man's best friend.

He couldn't think of any solution other than marrying Terry as soon as possible. That would still leave the problem of where they would live, but at least, wherever it was, they'd be able to share a bed. Unless her religion was a problem, but he didn't think so. He had no intention of converting to Catholicism, but he also had no objections to having a religious ceremony if that's what she wanted. And he was sure that would be what she wanted.

As for getting her father's approval, unless he was reading things wrong, Terry didn't approve of her father's girlfriend, so he didn't think it would matter if her father didn't approve of him. Not that he hadn't been friendly, but that baseball business hadn't endeared Wynn to him, if he wasn't mistaken.

He wasn't paying any attention to his fortune, just nodding and smiling during pauses, which appeared to satisfy Aunt Rosa. He had a feeling that he wasn't going to be alone with Terry for the rest of the weekend. He also had a feeling that he was going to need a couple of days off just to recover.

He had never realized how exhausting families could be.

AT FOUR O'CLOCK in the morning Terry was awakened by a noise on the deck. She sat up, remembered that Wynn was sleeping up there and yelled, "Are you all right?"

It was her brother whose head appeared in the door. "It's me, Terry. The boat leaves in twenty minutes."

"What boat?"

"I told you yesterday, I'm taking a party out this morning."

"It's not morning, Tony—it's the middle of the night. It's still dark out."

"You have to leave early to catch the fish."

"I don't remember your telling me this."

"I told you at least twice."

Terry got out of bed and faced him. "This is not going to work, Tony. I am not about to get up at this hour so that you can go out on my boat. I have to work, you know."

"When did you think I was going to use it?"

"At a reasonable hour, that's when."

"The men are going to be here any minute."

Wynn stuck his head around the door and said, "What's the problem?"

"The problem is, Tony expects us to leave the boat—he has customers coming."

"I'll get dressed," said Wynn, of no help to her at all.

ON THE DRIVE into the city, Wynn said, "I admire you, you know."

"Me?"

"Yes, you."

"Whatever for?"

"For living on that small boat with Mike and Henry; for living without hot water; for driving an open vehicle in all weather. In comparison, I'm afraid I'm decadent."

Terry laughed. "Oh, I imagine I like luxury as well as you do. Did I ever tell you I used to work out at the Y?"

"No. But I admire that, too."

"Don't. After Le Club, I don't think I'd ever be satisfied with the Y again."

"I'm crazy about you, you know."

She turned to look at him. "Even after this weekend?"

"I know it stretches credulity."

"Well, I'm crazy about you, too."

He was silent for a moment, then said, "Actually, if you want the truth, I'm more than crazy about you. I love you, Terry."

Her body reacted with a warmth a second before her mind took in the words. "I love you, too, Wynn. I also admire the way you put up with my family. I hadn't planned on springing that many of them on you at once."

"You mean there's more?" He sounded pleased, which had to be about her loving him, not about more family members.

"I'm afraid so. But you usually only see all of them at family gatherings."

"And the next one is?"

"July Fourth."

"The Fourth of July is wonderful on Fire Island. We even have our own fireworks display."

"So does Coney Island."

"We'll fight about it later. So what're we going to do? It's still dark out and we don't have to be at work for a couple of hours."

Terry reached for his hand. "I was thinking maybe you'd invite me over."

"I'll fix you breakfast."

"That wasn't what I had in mind."

"It wasn't what I had in mind, either, but I was trying to be polite."

"Don't be polite, just act normally," she said, treating him just like her son.

But there the resemblance ended.

Chapter Twelve

The consensus was in by noon. Four pro, two con, one abstention and two remaining to be polled.

Kathy had called first. She thought Wynn was marvelous, absolutely perfect, the best thing that had ever happened to Terry; Kathy was so overly approving that Terry thought maybe she should have doubts about him.

Joanna was heard from next. She made only a short call from her office, but she wanted to tell Terry how much she had liked Wynn.

"What did Tony think?" asked Terry.

"Oh, you know men. He thought Wynn seemed a little slick, which means he was impressed but doesn't know why."

Pop called promptly, then avoided the issue. When Terry asked him point-blank what he thought of Wynn, he kept saying things like, "Cindi thinks he's great," or "Cindi thinks he's interesting," which meant nothing to Terry, since Cindi didn't appear to have the brains to make a value judgment.

"But what did you think of him, Pop?" she asked, wondering why she still felt the need of her father's approval.

"He seemed nice enough, Terry."

"Nice enough? What does that mean?"

"He seemed like a good man. Not the kind I'd probably choose for a friend...."

"Why not?"

"Terry, he's different from us. Can you see him sitting out in the bleachers watching the Mets?"

"That's what you base friendship on?"

"Terry, I have nothing against the man. If you're happy with him, that's good enough for me."

None of that was of primary importance. What mattered was what Mike thought of him, and she wouldn't know that until Tony and Mike returned from fishing.

Wynn called shortly before noon and asked whether she'd have lunch with him if he came by.

"You just saw me a few hours ago," she reminded him.

"Seen enough of me lately, huh?"

"I didn't say that."

"So lunch is on?"

"Sure." It would be a treat. Usually she went down the block to the diner, but she knew Wynn would insist on someplace better.

He did. He took her to a restaurant where she was dressed worse than the waitresses, but that didn't bother her at all. She saw that Wynn didn't even notice. All he was looking at was her, and he wasn't even taking in the way she was dressed.

"I've decided we better get married right away," said Wynn as soon as they'd ordered.

"What?" Terry couldn't believe her ears.

"It's the only solution I can come up with. How else are we going to see each other?"

"Wynn, I can't rush into something like this."

"I know you love me. You told me so."

"Sure I love you, but I'm not entirely free. There are other considerations besides what I may want."

His eyes took on their slanty look, but at the same time he reached across the table and took her hand. "Your son doesn't like me, is that it?"

She thought of all the calls she'd gotten that morning and smiled. "I haven't talked to him yet, but most of the family was crazy about you."

"Did that include your father?"

He would have to bring that up. "Pop just wants me to be happy."

"Which is avoiding the question, but I'll let you get away with it. It was the baseball, wasn't it?"

"The whole family's crazy about the Mets."

"Including you?"

She nodded.

"Does that mean I'm going to have to spend the rest of my life watching baseball games?"

"Maybe," she said with a grin.

"It might drive me to drink."

She chuckled. "Lots of times I watch the games in bed."

"Oh, really?" He looked interested.

"It can be fun."

"I'll bet it can."

Any further observations were cut off by the arrival of their food, at which point Wynn got back to his original theme—marriage. "So how long do we have to wait? A couple of weeks?"

"Give Mike enough time to get used to you, Wynn. We haven't even known each other that long."

"Yes, but I keep thinking what'll happen when the case is solved and you're back on the boat all the time. How are we ever going to see each other?"

"You can spend some weekends on the boat and other times we'll come out to Fire Island," she said, although she could already imagine the arguments she'd get from Mike over that.

"And we'd each sleep alone."

"Not at all. You can sleep with Henry."

"I like your sense of humor, Terry, but do you know what you're asking of me?"

"Sure. It'll be just as hard on me. But if we want to get married there are going to be a lot of problems that have to be solved first. Even if Mike does like you, there's the matter of where we'll live."

"We can find a place in Manhattan where you won't have to commute so far."

"That'd be great, but Mike will want to finish next year at his school. I wouldn't think of taking him out before he graduates."

"Any other problems?"

"I like Pop being next door when Mike gets home from school. I know at his age he doesn't need babysitting, but it's still reassuring."

"We could afford a housekeeper, you know."

"Really?"

"Really." He smiled at her obvious delight. "Nothing's insurmountable, Terry. Remember that." It sounded good at the time, but that was before she had spoken to Mike.

"What difference does it make if I like him?" Mike asked. "I don't care if you like my dates. When I have them, that is."

"He's not just a date, Mike."

"No? How long've you known him, Mom?"

"Awhile."

"Not that long if you met him at that health club you're going to. How's the case coming? You going to be back home soon?"

She wasn't sure if he was trying to get off the subject of Wynn or whether he was really interested, so she said, "Not too well, Mike. But I don't think I'll be kept on decoy indefinitely. If something doesn't break this week, there's talk of closing down Le Club."

"Good. Then you'll be home again."

"Wynn has a house at the beach, Mike—on Fire Island."

"So what?"

"Would you like to go out there some weekend?"

"What for?"

"I thought you might enjoy the beach."

"We live on the water, why do I need a beach? You think I'm going to lay out there and try to get a tan like girls do?"

Terry sighed. "Would you spend a weekend there if I asked you to?"

"Come on, Mom. What would I do?"

"What if you could bring a friend along?"

"Yeah, maybe. Do we have to talk about it now? You haven't even asked how the fishing went."

"How'd it go?"

"It was great, Mom. The men even gave me tips. I figure I'll have enough saved up by the end of the summer to buy a motor for our rowboat."

Terry thought of telling him Wynn would probably buy him a whole damn motorboat if he'd just come around, but bribery wasn't a good basis for a relationship, so she didn't.

That night, which was usually the busiest night at Le Club, the place was almost deserted. Attendance wasn't helped by a series of scare articles the *Post* was running, although Terry hadn't thought the members of Le Club were the type to read the *Post*.

She couldn't blame the women for not coming. Even Lisa wasn't there, and she had thought her friend would be the last holdout.

She could have been invisible for all the attention paid to her by the men there. If the strangler was among their ranks, she didn't think she was next in line. Maybe it would be better to close down the place. Maybe it wouldn't stop him from killing women, but it might force him into making mistakes. So far, he hadn't made any.

Wynn hadn't come to the club, but he'd told her he'd probably have to work late. She hadn't been home ten minutes when he showed up, a huge bunch of daisies in his hands.

"I love them, but why?" she asked, taking them from him and finding a vase—an art deco vase, naturally, which didn't seem to go with daisies at all.

"I'm going to propose again," he told her, dragging her by the hand to sit next to him on the couch. The temperature had hit an unseasonable 100° that day and even the shaded yard wouldn't offer any relief.

"I didn't say no, Wynn. I just said we couldn't rush it."

"That scares me. I see you moving back on your boat and never having time to see me and finally, I guess, the whole thing just petering out."

She put her arm across his chest and leaned her face against his. "Wynn, I'm not going to stop loving you. I couldn't even imagine life without you now."

"I guess it's just that now that I've decided I don't want to live alone anymore, I don't feel like waiting. What did Mike have to say?"

"He'll get used to the idea in time."

"How can you be so sure of that? Parents often think that about their kids, and a lot of the time they're wrong."

"He might be jealous, and he might resent you at first, but I know he loves me and eventually he'll want whatever makes me happy."

"You're talking about a kid, Terry. Kids put their own happiness first."

"I'd still rather not force it on him. How can he help but like you when he gets to know you?"

"I can think of a lot of people I haven't liked when I got to know them."

"Give me the summer, all right? At the end of the summer, if Tony's business is still going on, I'll let him have the boat and we can find a larger place."

"In Brooklyn?"

"Would you mind very much?"

"For you I'd live in New Jersey. If I had to."

"You probably know New Jersey about as well as you know Brooklyn. There are very nice sections of both."

"All right," he said, folding his arms around her. "I didn't come over here to argue with you."

"What did you come over for?"

"For one of your submarine sandwiches, what else?"

IN A FREAK ACCIDENT on Wednesday night, Terry got tripped up on the track and managed to twist her ankle rather badly. Wynn, whom she had persuaded to run rather than use the exercycles, was right behind her and quickly helped her to her feet, then supported her with his arm.

"How's it feel?" he asked, looking more worried than she thought was warranted. Mostly she was just feeling clumsy.

"I just twisted it," she said, pushing his arm away.

"Maybe we better get you home."

She gave him a warning look. "I'll go home—you can come by later if you want. Now go on running."

"Terry—" he said, starting to argue, but she glared at him.

"Right now, Wynn. You know I'm not supposed to be seeing you here."

He glared right back at her for a few seconds, then reluctantly took off around the track.

Terry limped down the stairs, and since Le Club was virtually empty, Scott spotted her right away and came over to her. "What happened?" he asked.

"Don't worry, Scott, I'm not going to sue. I just twisted it. It'll be okay once I rest it."

He squatted down and felt her ankle, then nodded. "Nothing broken. What you should do is go home and put some ice on it."

"Thanks," she told him. "See you tomorrow night."

Halfway home her ankle felt better and she debated turning back, then decided she might as well take an evening off from exercising. Since she knew Wynn would be by, and since she had the makings of lasagna in the refrigerator, she thought she'd surprise him with dinner.

She was just setting out the ingredients when the doorbell rang, and planning on chiding him for cutting his workout so short, she opened the door and was almost speaking when she saw that it was Scott, not Wynn.

"Oh, hi," she said. "If you were worried about my ankle, it's okay now. I guess I shouldn't have left so fast."

He was in the door before she could stop him and that's when she wondered how he knew her address. She was about to ask him when he unzipped the bag he was carrying and dragged out something, saying, "I brought over a heating pad for you. Even if your ankle feels all right, I don't think it would hurt to use it."

She was feeling a rush of adrenaline and was wondering why, when she realized that he could be the strangler and she had just let him in. "How'd you know where I lived, Scott?" she asked, wondering why her body seemed to be reacting while her mind was telling her it wasn't possible. Not Scott.

He gave her an easy smile. "I looked it up at the desk. Since you were so close, I figured I'd run by. The place is dead tonight anyway."

She was beginning to think it was paranoia. She had always liked Scott. He was friendly and nice and had a sense of humor, and he sure wasn't hard to look at, either. But he had gotten into her apartment with ease, and she thought he probably could have managed the same thing with almost any of the members.

To be on the safe side, she mentally located her gun, which would be in her handbag on one of the chairs in the kitchen. Acting casual, she walked toward the kitchen, saying to Scott, "I was just going to have a beer, would you like one?"

Thankfully he didn't follow her, just said, "No, thanks, I have to go back to work."

With her back to him so he couldn't see what she was doing if he was looking, she reached into her purse and put the gun in the waistband of her jeans. She pulled her T-shirt over it. The bulge was noticeable, so she crossed her arms to mask it.

She turned back to the living room saying, "Well, thanks, Scott, I'll return it tomorrow night."

He was leaning against the door, his own arms crossed. "I admire you, you know," he said. "You're one of the few female members who still comes and is even halfway friendly."

"I might be halfway friendly, but I'm still careful."

Then he said something that froze her blood. "We're not supposed to talk about this, but we've been working with the police on the case and they think they know who it is."

"Oh?" she said. "Is it anyone I know?"

He was still acting so casual and friendly that she had trouble believing what she was hearing. "I don't think so. I see you talking to Wynn Ransome a lot, and it's not him."

"Was he there tonight?" She wanted to keep him talking, maybe get him to make a move. So far, he'd only given himself away by saying he was cooperating with the police, which, he could always claim later, was just bragging. And maybe it was, but she was getting a funny feeling about him.

"No way. If he had been there, I wouldn't have left. All of us who work there are keeping an eye on him. So what's with you and Ransome? You two seeing each other?"

She didn't see any point in lying. "Yeah, we've been out a few times."

"Figures. That's the type the women seem to go for."

"He's a nice man," said Terry.

"Sure. And it also helps that he has bucks."

Terry wondered why he didn't sense anything, why he didn't find it strange that she was just standing there with her arms crossed. She didn't know how much longer she could keep it up. Maybe if she made him angry in some way he would act, so remembering something Lisa had once said, she said, "I don't see why I should date someone who makes less money than I do. I don't feel like getting stuck with the check."

He gave her such a look of disappointment she was sure she had been wrong, and she began to feel guilty for thinking the worst of him.

But that guilt didn't last long, because his disappointment quickly turned to anger. "You're all the same," he said, and she could see his muscles tensing.

"I'm sure you do all right, Scott."

"Do you think I have a good body?"

She couldn't imagine that he thought this was a normal conversation they were having. For her part, if she weren't a cop she'd have been terrified by this point. "You have a perfect body," she told him.

"It didn't just happen, you know. To have a body like mine takes years of work."

"I know. But it was worth it, wasn't it?"

"What's the point? You figure if you've got the best body around, women are going to go for you. Isn't that what you'd think?"

She nodded, scarcely breathing.

"Yeah, that's what everyone thinks. Well, think again! The women at Le Club are only interested in one thing—success. Oh, they might go out with me once or twice. But they're all looking for the main chance. All a guy like Wynn Ransome has to do is lift a finger, and goodbye, Scott."

Unfortunately, Terry knew that was true. She also knew she couldn't just stand there much longer. He might be capable of talking on and on, but she was getting too nervous. "So what do you do about it, Scott? Strangle them?"

WYNN HATED RUNNING. He had done it a couple of times at Terry's insistence, but once she left he switched to the exercycles.

He was just about finished with his twenty minutes when he saw one of the women from the desk in the lobby come hurrying out of the elevator and make a beeline for Kyle.

He was just getting off the cycle when he saw Kyle take off for the elevators at a run. Since Wynn was halfway there, he stopped Kyle and said, "Is something the matter?"

"Stay out of this, Ransome," warned Kyle.

"Has it got anything to do with Terry?"

"She's a cop; she's trained to handle this," said Kyle, which was enough to make Wynn's blood pressure rise at an alarming rate.

Ignoring Kyle's warning, ignoring the fact that he was in his workout clothes, Wynn followed Kyle out of the building, then took off at a run after him. He didn't need to have it spelled out. He had seen Terry leave. Minutes later he had seen Scott leave. He had wondered about it at the time, had felt uneasy and now was no longer wondering. Terry was in danger and he wasn't going to wait around to hear about it later.

Instead of going straight to Terry's door, as Wynn had expected, Kyle ran into the lobby of the hotel. "Will you please tell me what's happening?" Wynn yelled at him.

Kyle turned to him, seemed about to tell him to get lost again, then appeared to think better of it. "One of the women at the desk told me Scott asked for Terry's home address. Terry knows how to handle herself, but if you want to help—"

"Of course I want to help."

"Okay. Give me three minutes to get into her yard, then start banging on her door. I figure that'll get his attention long enough for me to get a drop on him."

"You got it," said Wynn, wondering how he was going to survive those three minutes.

He went outside and positioned himself in front of Terry's door, wishing he knew what was going on inside. What he wanted to do, was tempted to do, was just to break her door down, but a good look at it told him it would be a futile gesture. He could work out for the next thirty years and still not be able to break down a steel door.

He kept telling himself she was a cop, she was armed, she knew how to handle something like this. But he didn't believe it. All he could think of was the fact that she was half Scott's size, had probably been taken by surprise and, right now, at this very minute, Scott could be strangling her and he was helpless to do anything about it.

But if she was okay, he knew one thing. She was going to be with him from now on, and if her son didn't like it, that was too damn bad.

TERRY HAD SEEN criminals break down before, but seldom as quickly as it had happened with Scott.

One moment he had been raving about his body, asking her what it was that women wanted. The next he was alternately crying with remorse and screaming with rage, his handsome features contorted to where she wouldn't have recognized him.

Somewhere in the middle of all this, she had drawn her gun and taken the safety off. He didn't appear to notice it pointed at him, but it made her feel better. There was no way she was going to be able to overpower him and get the cuffs on him, but there was also no way he was going to be able to strangle her. She hoped it wouldn't come to shooting him. She had never shot anyone and never wanted to have to, but if it came down to her life or his, she knew she wouldn't hesitate.

Their confrontation had just reached the bizarre point where Scott was ripping off his shirt, wanting to show her his perfect body—the one the other women, according to him, had rejected—when there came a pounding at the front door and at the same time Kyle came charging in from the yard, his gun held in both hands the way they had taught them at the police academy.

Kyle took in the scene, lowered the gun and said, "You get a confession out of him?"

"It's still going on," said Terry, relaxing a little as Scott, on his knees now and seemingly oblivious, was allowing Kyle to handcuff him.

"Who's at the door—backup?" Terry asked.

"It's your boyfriend. He was worried about you."

Terry found herself smiling as she circled Scott and Kyle and opened the door.

Wynn sagged with relief when he saw her. "I thought you were dead," he told her, pulling her into his arms.

"I'm okay." Shaking maybe, but okay.

"I saw him follow you out and I should've done something, but it just didn't register."

"No reason it should've," said Terry. "You're not a cop."

Kyle was pulling Scott to his feet. "We'll take your Jeep, Terry—you drive." If she got to drive, that must mean she was now going to be treated by Kyle as one of the guys.

"Can I go with you?" asked Wynn.

She gave him a hug, then backed out of his arms. "Go on home, Wynn. I'll call you when it's over. It's going to be a long night."

"Is there anything I can do?"

She smiled up at him. "Oh, I can think of several things, but they're going to have to wait."

She was getting her handbag and putting her gun back into it when Wynn said, "Just one thing, Terry."

"Yes?"

"We're getting married immediately."

Kyle, a look of exasperation on his face, said, "Okay, let's knock off the romance, you two. You got the rest of your lives for that."

Terry held the door open for Kyle and Scott, then waited for Wynn to precede her. Just before she left to follow Kyle to the Jeep, she said, "This weekend."

"What?"

She smiled. "We'll get married this weekend. It'll be like a surprise party. Mike's always loved surprise parties."

Wynn was looking as if he liked surprise parties, too.

Epilogue

It was October before escrow closed and they were able to move into the old Victorian house on the tree-lined street in Brooklyn Heights.

Wynn, who would have placed the whole job into the hands of professional movers, watched instead as Terry's entire family turned out to help with the moving.

Pop had shown up at dawn at Wynn's co-op, which was going to be sublet until the day when he and Terry might want to live in the city. His father-in-law had rented a U-Haul, and ignoring the looks from the doorman and the concierge, Wynn and he had carried down the furniture in the service elevator. Since their marriage, Wynn, Terry and Mike had been spending weekends in the city or on Fire Island, the rest of the week in crowded quarters on her boat. Very crowded quarters. Mike slept in one bunk, Terry in the other, and Wynn slept on a folding cot they had bought, most often with Henry sleeping across his feet.

Pop had kept up a running commentary as they moved up and down the elevator. He said things like,

"It'll be better now that you have some space," and "Mike's going to love living in a real house," and "Tony can really get going now with that charter-boat business of his."

Wynn agreed with it all, but didn't really get a chance to comment. Terry's father was a nonstop talker when he put his mind to it. Pop and he had become friends, his profession somewhat forgiven by both Pop and Mike when they found that in addition to designing clothes, he could also play poker and draw a mean Superman.

The space part was going to be the most important. Three of them on the boat during the week hadn't endeared Wynn to Mike, but, surprisingly, the weekends in Manhattan had worked out fine. Sometimes Mike was allowed to bring a friend along, and the two of them always had a good time in Central Park. And when he didn't bring a friend, he seemed to enjoy seeing the city with his mother and Wynn. And Fire Island had been a real hit. Mike found friends there right away, and Henry had enthusiastically taken to running on the beach and even plunging into the water for a swim. Wynn had grown to like Terry's father and to enjoy having a kid around. Henry, though, he was nuts about. He couldn't understand how he could have gone through life never having a dog.

Mike hadn't taken to calling him Dad or anything even close, but Wynn thought they were becoming friends. And in return for Mike's agreeing to add some cultural experiences to his life, Wynn had agreed to install a basketball net over the garage and let Mike teach him the fine art of one-on-one. He was pretty sure that in the spring he'd be coerced into playing baseball, but found himself looking forward to it. He didn't think he and Terry would have the time for Le Club anymore, so any exercise he got would be a help.

All in all, he thought, moving furniture might not be his idea of a great time, but marrying Terry had been the best move he had ever made.

TERRY HAD ALSO BEEN up at dawn. Her brother, with the help of Mike, had loaded all her things into his pickup to take to the new house, and Joanna, Cindi and Kathy were over at the house cleaning it in preparation.

The house was more than a dream come true for Terry. Never, in her wildest imagining, had she ever thought she'd live in a real house with three floors and a front porch and a backyard big enough for Henry.

"But I don't know a thing about interior decorating," she said to Wynn when their offer had been accepted and she believed for the first time that they'd actually be moving into the house.

"You don't have to," he said. "We'll just fill it with things we love. And there's no hurry. It doesn't matter if it takes the rest of our lives to furnish it."

Terry loved the size of the house. It was ridiculously big for three people, but just right for holidays when no one in her family had the room to seat everyone for dinner. She could picture Christmas with her whole family around her, and they'd have a guest room for Wynn's mother when she visited them from Florida. There would be room for a huge Christmas tree and a yard where all the kids could have snowball fights.

She was still dreaming about Christmas when Tony turned onto her street and she saw the trees on her block with their leaves all turning, making it look more like the country than Brooklyn. She found herself holding her breath until she saw her house, then picturing it with snow on the ground and candles in the windows.

"What a great place to go out trick-or-treating," said Mike. His statement reminded her that Halloween, not Christmas, would be the next holiday, and she switched her thoughts to pumpkins in the windows and maybe a skeleton hung on the front door.

"You don't mind moving?" she asked him.

"Mind? I think it's great. My friends are going to freak out when they see this place."

Kathy was sweeping the front porch when they pulled up and parked, and she ran down the steps and gave Terry a hug. "This house is just incredible," she was saying. "Cindi's in there telling Joanna she'd like one just like it, but I can't see Pop moving off the boat, can you?"

Terry wasn't so sure. A few months of living next to Pop and Cindi had shown her that there wasn't much her father wouldn't do for the young woman. He was becoming so domesticated she hardly recognized him at times. It was a good change, though, and Terry was glad for her father, since she wouldn't be close by anymore. She still wasn't crazy about Cindi, who, at her early age, was now getting into an Italian mother act, giving Terry and Kathy advice as though it had been culled from years of experience. Cindi at a few miles' distance, though, was going to be easier to take than Cindi right next door.

Terry was still worried about Kathy, but she and Johnny were seeing a marriage counselor and maybe something good would come of it. And even if it didn't, Kathy was now enrolled at Brooklyn College, calling herself the oldest freshman in history, and no longer had the time to nag at her kids, or at a husband if Johnny and she got together again.

They had finished unloading the pickup and were all sitting around on the living room floor when Pop and Wynn arrived. Mike went charging out of the house, yelling, "Wynn, when're we going to put up the basketball net?" Terry, standing in the doorway, saw him smile at her over Mike's head.

"You're lucky," said Kathy, coming up behind her.

"I know," said Terry.

"No luckier than me," said Wynn, leaning down and kissing Terry.

"Let's get our priorities right," said Mike, a phrase he had picked up from Wynn. "Basketball first, then kissing."

Wynn put one arm around Terry's shoulders and the other around Mike's. "You got a lot to learn, kid," he said.

When Mike didn't flinch away from the embrace, Terry knew everything was going to be all right.

Harlequin American Romance

COMING NEXT MONTH

#169 WHEN HEARTS COLLIDE by Ginger Chambers

Ominous noises. Creaking doors. Rachel had worked at the famed Aspenridge Hotel without encountering a hint of the supernatural until Jared and his three aunts arrived. They loved to imagine disturbances in the silence. Rachel could deal with this. The impossible was being haunted by the living in the shape of one Jared Donnelly.

#170 TO TOUCH THE STARS by Pamela Browning

In Peaceable Kingdom, GA, people were walking on air. Julie Andrassy watched as her relatives fell under the spell of Stephen Martinovic, the dashing émigré who dreamed of reuniting the Amazing Andrassys on the high wire. Could Julie remain earthbound, refusing to admit that Stephen and the high wire were twin fires in her blood?

#171 I LOVE YOU, JONATHAN SKY by Anne Henry

As a public figure in the San Diego medical community, Beth couldn't afford to make a mistake. Public figures couldn't expect to have private lives—or private affairs. Before Beth could allow herself to fall for Johnathan Sky, the brilliant cardiology resident, she had to be sure she had the strength to put her own happiness first.

#172 OPEN CHANNELS by Rebecca Bond

Amelia knew that hard work and diligence got you anything. It took a couple of years, but the perfect job came. Scott, whose ambition was to find the perfect wave on which to ride his Windsurfer, came into her life and gave her love. It seemed a perfect situation until Amelia was faced with something that she'd always wanted.

OFFICIAL RULES

Harlequin "Super Celebration" SWEEPSTAKES

NEW PRIZES—NEW PRIZE FEATURES & CHOICES—MONTHLY

1. To enter the sweepstakes, follow the instructions outlined on the Center Insert Card. Alternate means of entry, NO PURCHASE NECESSARY, you may also enter by mailing your name, address and birthday on a plain 3" x 5" piece of paper to: In U.S.A.: Harlequin "Super Celebration" Sweepstakes, P.O. Box 1867, Buffalo, N.Y. 14240-1867. In Canada: Harlequin "Super Celebration" Sweepstakes, P.O. Box 2800, 5170 Yonge Street, Postal Station A, Willowdale, Ontario M2N 6J3.

2. Winners will be selected in random drawings from all entries received. All prizes will be awarded. These prizes are in addition to any free gifts which might be offered. Versions of this sweepstakes with different prizes may appear in other presentations by TorStar and their affiliates. The maximum value of the prizes offered is $8,000.00. Winners selected will receive the prize offered from their prize package.

3. The selection of winners will be conducted under the supervision of Marden-Kane, an independent judging organization. By entering the sweepstakes, each entrant accepts and agrees to be bound by these rules and the decision of the judges which shall be final and binding. Odds of winning are dependent upon the total number of entries received. Taxes, if any, are the sole responsibility of the winners. Prizes are not transferable. This sweepstakes is scheduled to appear in Retail Outlets of Harlequin Books during the period of June 1986 to December 1986. All entries must be received by January 31st, 1987. The drawing will take place on or about March 1st, 1987 at the offices of Marden-Kane, Lake Success, New York. For Quebec (Canada) residents, any litigation regarding the running of this sweepstakes and the awarding of prizes must be submitted to La Regie de Lotteries et Course du Quebec.

4. This presentation offers the prizes as illustrated on the Center Insert Card.

5. This offer is open to residents of the U.S., and Canada, 18 years or older, except employees of TorStar, its affilliates, subsidiaries, Marden-Kane and all other agencies and persons connected with conducting this sweepstakes. All Federal, State and local laws apply. Void where prohibited or restricted by law. Winners will be notified by mail and may be required to execute an affidavit of eligibility and release which must be returned within 14 days after notification. Winners consent to the use of their name, photograph and/or likeness for advertising and publicity in conjunction with this and similar promotions without additional compensation. One prize per family or household. Canadian winners will be required to answer a skill testing question.

6. For a list of our most recent prize winners, send a stamped, self-addressed envelope to: WINNERS LIST, c/o Marden-Kane, P.O. Box 525, Sayreville, NJ 08872.

No Lucky Number needed to win!

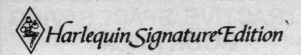

Harlequin Signature Edition

Violet Winspear

THE HONEYMOON

Blackmailed into marriage, a reluctant bride discovers intoxicating passion and heartbreaking doubt.

Is it Jorja or her resemblance to her sister that stirs Renzo Talmonte's desire?

A turbulent love story unfolds in the glorious tradition of Violet Winspear, *la grande dame* of romance fiction.

Available in October wherever paperbacks are sold, or send your name, address and zip or postal code, along with a check or money order for $4.00 (includes 75¢ for postage and handling) payable to Harlequin Reader Service, to:

HARLEQUIN READER SERVICE

In the U.S.
P.O. Box 1392
Buffalo, NY
14240

In Canada
P.O. Box 609
Fort Erie, Ontario
L2A 9Z9

ATTRACTIVE, SPACE SAVING BOOK RACK

Display your most prized novels on this handsome and sturdy book rack. The hand-rubbed walnut finish will blend into your library decor with quiet elegance, providing a practical organizer for your favorite hard-or soft-covered books.

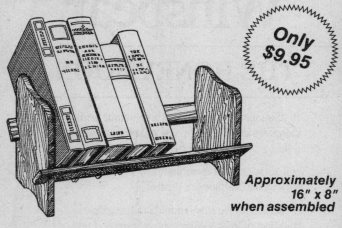

Only $9.95

Approximately 16" x 8" when assembled

Assembles in seconds!

To order, rush your name, address and zip code, along with a check or money order for $10.70 ($9.95 plus 75¢ postage and handling) (New York residents add appropriate sales tax), payable to *Harlequin Reader Service* to:

In the U.S.

Harlequin Reader Service
Book Rack Offer
901 Fuhrmann Blvd.
P.O. Box 1325
Buffalo, NY 14269-1325

Offer not available in Canada.